ROGUE ROBOT BOOK 2

CYBS

MEG FOSTER

Meg Foster
Copyrighted Material

CYBS
© 2021 by Meg Foster. All rights reserved.

Paperback Edition ISBN: 978-1-954902-01-5

www.MegFoster.com

1st Edition

Cover Art by Deranged Doctor Design
Editing by Paula Lester, Polaris Editing
Published by Foster On Media LLC

Books by Meg Foster

Rogue Robot Series:

ROBOTS DON'T CRY (prequel novella ebook)*
ROGUE (Book 1)
CYBS (Book 2)
JUSTICE (Book 3)
HARMONIX (Book 4)
TRINITY (Book 5)
CODA (Book 6)

*Only available when signing up for
Meg's newsletter.

This series is meant to be read in order.

CONTENTS

1

———

Dr. Goggins guided the red-hot repair fuser on my back shoulder armor. I hoped he wouldn't slip.

He slipped. "Ahh!" I yelled.

"Gabe, you big sissy." He yanked the fuser away. "Why don't you pull down your pain sensors, so we can accomplish these repairs easier?"

"No. Keep going. I'll be okay," I said.

Dr. Goggins sighed and resumed repairing the damage I had received in a fight against Heragi Empire military-bots at the rebel base on the planet of Zaradorba.

You see, I'm a robot.

A rogue robot. I'm able to kill humans upon my discretion. That's what makes me rogue. Illegal robot code that the Heragi Empire outlawed. Drs. Ava and Damiel Kell enabled me to kill humans, which other bots mostly can't. Only military and police-bots can, when given the order, and I'm neither of those. No one has to order me.

Don't be scared of me though. I don't indiscriminately kill humans. Only when they are trying to kidnap or hurt the Kells' children. Or my shipmates. Or anyone I don't believe should be hurt by the Heragi Empire. So that isn't a large number or anything. So far, that is.

And I can feel pain. The Kells imbedded synthetic pain sensors throughout my body. Their theory was that it would help me empathize with humans — specifically their three children whom I was given a mission to save and protect.

The pain subsided, and I knew Dr. Goggins had completed his repairs.

"Okay, big boy, all done," he said, slapping my back.

I rose and loomed over him, just to scare him a bit. It worked. Goggins crouched away from my large frame.

"Thank you." I walked out of the medbay and back to the bridge. What can I tell you about Goggins? He's both brilliant and annoying, as the Kells would say. I agree. But for the most part, he has shown his allegiance to me and the rebel resistance, and his navigational skills are stellar. I know this since he worked at the Ameribot Labs back on Heragi with the Kells as their assistant, and he coded my navigational programs.

I sat down in the commander chair on our spaceship, the *Alyssia*.

We were docked at the Charbeaux Station, a trading post in an unchartered sector of our galaxy, which means it was not under the Heragi Empire control. It also means it was a bit unruly or *seedy,* as Goggins described it.

"Feti, do you have updated information on when the Kell children will be here?" I asked.

"Yes, Gabe. They will arrive in four hours and ten minutes," it said.

Feti is our ship's AI. It controls the systems of the *Alyssia*. He's a bit shy, but we've bonded since we've met or, I should say, since I stole the *Alyssia* out of a planet-port on Heragi when I saved the Kell children. As our ship's system manager, Feti is most helpful and accommodating.

"Thank you, Feti."

Light footsteps came toward the bridge. It must be Zara, based on the pace and weight of the steps.

She plopped down in the co-commander seat opposite me. "I feel like my eyeballs are about to explode looking at all that data."

I scanned her eyes. They did look bloodshot, but I realized she was exaggerating, the way most humans do. "Did you run it through Feti? It could help you with the analysis," I said.

"No, I've got scripts running through it. I want to make sure nothing is missed, so I'm doing spot checking too." She pounded on her hand coder.

Zara was sorting through recent comm relays between starships and planetary systems that we downloaded from a nearby satellite. We were hoping to find out where our friend, Synthia, was kidnapped to by a scientist named Stefano, who worked under the Heragi Empire.

Zara was an expert hacker, but she needed time to review the comm relays to see if Stefano slipped up and left a trace about what planet he was traveling to with Synthia. Zara was anxious. I got it. Nobody wanted Synthia harmed. And none of us wanted Stefano to keep manipulating Synthia's telepathic skills for the Heragi Empire's alliance with the Suissey planet's financial monopoly to rule the galaxy or to harm any rebels.

One other item, Synthia can do more than just relay thoughts to other telepaths — she can also break into people's minds and tell if they are lying and then offer up the names or locations they are trying to hide from Heragi interrogators. And when Stefano drugs Synthia, which he has done in the past, there is a possibility that he will manipulate her to give up rebel names.

Yes, we needed to reach her as fast as possible.

Goggins entered the bridge.

My crew and I had been hiding out at the Charbeaux Station, waiting to plan our next move to find Synthia.

I reviewed our supply systems. Although the owner of the

Alyssia, tech mogul Edward Gates, had done a fine job keeping inventory high on most items, I didn't think he could have predicted a crew hijacking his spaceship and running through the ammo and torpedoes as fast as we had in our last battle. We needed more ammo, since I didn't think Stefano would give up Synthia with just diplomatic tidings.

"Who would like to accompany me to pick up supplies at the station?" I asked.

"I've got to keep crunching this code," said Zara.

"I thought you would never ask. I've been itching to see what it looks like there, if what I've heard is true," said Goggins.

"What do you believe you'll find?" asked Zara.

"I heard you can buy anything exotic and wild at the Charbeaux Station. The only limit is a person's galaxy card," he said as he pulled out his hologram credit card. "Mine has a negative balance, so I guess I'll only be a spectator." Goggins pouted.

Zara ran her fingers over her coder and glanced over to Goggins with a smirk. "Check your card now."

Goggins looked down, and he saw number signs changing on its hologram screen, going in a positive direction. He now had thousands of credits that Zara had just siphoned from the Suissey government's banking system into Goggins' galaxy account. I was sure they wouldn't miss it.

A smile grew on Goggins' face. "Zara, did I ever tell you how crazy mad your coding skills are?"

"Countless times at school. And yeah, they are. Have fun," she said as she went back to reviewing her mounds of comm data to try to decipher where Synthia could be right now.

"I will. And if I see anything enticing for you, I will be sure to bring it back to the ship," he said.

"Um, don't. In fact, I'll put more credits in your account if you promise not to," she said.

"I promise," he said in a snap.

Zara's fingers flew across her coder again, and more galaxy

credit numbers ran upward on Goggins' card. He squealed with delight.

His high-pitched squawk hurt my ears. "Okay, let's go," I said, shaking my head.

We exited through the airlock at our hangar and caught the elevator to take us into the heart of Charbeaux Station. The elevator opened, and we were fifteen stories high, overlooking the station.

Goggins led the way. His excitement was not being contained. "This way, Gabe. Don't dawdle."

The station was impressive. Inside were hovertrams that went in every direction, intersected by an extensive elevator system that crisscrossed in a maze before us. Air taxis picked up shoppers, and visitors and residents were dropped off at hundreds of stores, restaurants and entertainment centers that lined the neon-signed sections of the station.

Aliens, humans and bots mixed freely.

You could tell the first-time tourists, like Goggins, whose mouths hung open at the sights of performers, magicians and barkers trying to round up business for their establishments. There were bars, singing stations and cafes on every block. Electronics, robots and hovercrafts were plentifully in stock and cheap.

Goggins picked up a robotic version of a cicichimp animal that Talia, the youngest of the Kell children, had adopted on one of the planet stops we made on our last mission. It cuddled Goggins as soon as it saw his interest. "Look! Talia would love this," he said as he petted the small furry animatronic imitation.

"She has a *real* cicichimp. Why would she want a replica?" I asked.

"When people love something, they want more and more of it. Real or fake. You don't know anything about being a human, do you?" He paid the furball's merchant and put the toy on his shoulder where it perched and softly pecked at his head. Goggins was like a kid in a candy store.

I thought of that phrase. *Kid in a candy store.* Ava must have coded it in my lexicon. If she put it there, I might as well use it. Not that she cared right now what I did.

She was mad at me. I saved her children and delivered them to their rebel leader uncle, Jebediah Kell, but I put them in harm's way on our journey, and she hadn't forgiven me. At least recently that seemed to be the case. I didn't blame her, I guess. The children were in danger. But I had determined the risk and decided to proceed. Maybe one day she would forgive me.

We entered the Charbeaux Station to power shop.

Goggins eyed the assortment of alien creatures that were trying to entice him into dark bars with music beating so hard it vibrated my armor. He let the creatures try to convince him to enter their establishments and then he shyly sauntered away, blushing. I didn't know how much more of this I could take. I was done.

"Dr. Goggins, this way to the armory warehouse," I said, turning a corner.

Goggins followed me with a frown. "Fine," he said as the cicichimp combed through his hair.

I found the armory and strode in. The alien heading the counter had six arms sprouting off a shimmering blue torso. I scanned its body and found an alien match in my directory. It was a Wasopola, and they were known for their warring planet and affinity for guns. With five of its arms, it showcased various guns and lasers, and with its sixth arm, it held its merchant scanner.

I approached it. "I need a load of torpedoes and deflectors for our ship."

"What's the name of your ship?" it asked.

"The *Alyssia*."

Goggins rolled his eyes and muttered, "Oh, no."

I wasn't making a mistake by giving the name of our stolen ship to the armory merchant. Edward Gates knew we had his ship. If this six-armed gunslinger was going to report us — who was it going to report us to? This was a station filled with thieves, con artists and runaways.

The merchant didn't lift even one of its five furry eyebrows at me when I said the ship's name. It just put all its guns down and typed into its arm comm.

"Nice ship, the *Alyssia,*" it said as three of its five eyes looked up at me.

"Yes, we like it," I replied.

"Okay, I got your engine requirements for the caliber you need. That will be twenty thousand galaxy credits. You got that?" It put all six arms down on the counter.

I pulled out my galaxy card, onto which Zara had loaded credits, and handed it to the merchant. It snatched the card and scanned it. The amount cleared, and it handed me back the card a bit more politely.

"I'll have it delivered to your gate in two hours," it said.

I nodded.

"Thank you," said Goggins as his head bobbed and weaved, not knowing which of the five Wasopola eyes he should be looking at.

"You know, I don't get many robots with their own galaxy card. In fact, I have never had a robot buy its own weapons before," it said as it picked up guns with all six arms and waved them nonchalantly in the air.

"There can be a first time for anything, I reckon." I stared at it hard.

"I reckon," repeated the merchant as it wandered off to help another customer.

Goggins and I exited out of the armory. He ran in front of me and stopped.

"Do you have to be so…what's the word? Hokey?"

"Hokey? You think I'm hokey?" I asked.

"The words you use. Can't you be more robotic? So no one finds out you have synthetic human neurons in you and rogue code?" He whispered so passing shoppers wouldn't hear him.

"Ava programmed my language. You know that. You were in the lab with the Kells when they built me. You helped them build me," I retorted. I felt defensive. *I am who I am.*

"She programmed *I reckon* in you?"

"Yes," I said.

"I'll have to have a *word* with her next time I see her," Goggins said, walking off ahead of me.

"I *reckon* you will," I said in a hushed tone.

Goggins continued his sightseeing on the station with me tagging along. My arm comm flashed, and a notification came up in my visor view. It was coming from our ship. I linked Goggins to the comm so he could listen in.

"Yeah, this is Gabe," I said.

"It's Zara. I got something," she said. "There was a comm relayed in this vicinity four days ago to Heragi. It was cleverly encrypted, but I hacked it. Most of the wording I don't understand. Some kind of private code language they must use, but three words stood out. They must be planets or coordinates of some kind."

Goggins spoke into his arm comm to Zara. "Have you run it through Feti yet?"

"Yeah, nothing pulled up in its logs," she said. "Want to have a crack?"

"I'm not too familiar with uncharted quadrants farther out. This station is on the edge of my knowledge base," he said.

"We need to find someone who may know which planet this message is referring to," she said. "And we need to find them quick."

Hundreds of bodies pushed past us on the street, coming and going to all the destination points on the station.

Goggins smiled. "I think I know where we can get some local intel. Meet us on the fourth level at a bar called the Blue Edger, pronto."

"Copy that," she said.

"What or who do you think you will find at the Blue Edger?" I asked.

Goggins smiled and pointed at a large neon sign of a spaceship with a blue alien drinking a cocktail. "It's a pilot bar. You know — a bar for pilots. You're a pilot." He laughed. "Never mind. We have to find a pilot who knows more about uncharted deep space than any navigation system we have access to." He took off down the street with the imitation cicichimp on his shoulder.

Goggins was right. If we could find an experienced pilot to help us, that would be wonderful. But I was not sure Goggins was going to make a lot of friends with a ridiculous cicichimp on his shoulder. I mean, it wasn't even a real one.

I followed Goggins down the street to the Blue Edger.

2

———————

Goggins and I entered the Blue Edger bar.

It was dark inside except for the glowing white bar and the floating ball lights above the high-top tables. Alien and human pilots were patrons of the bar. They swayed and swapped stories as they drank every drink imaginable out of illuminated glasses.

We found an open table and took a seat. The waiter, an alien of the Gorba species, approached us. His three eyes were red with unruly eyebrows, and his hair was perfectly combed back into a ponytail.

"What can I get you?" he asked.

Goggins slapped his hands and rubbed them together. "What do you recommend, my friend?"

I didn't honestly think Goggins had many friends. I held my tongue. Well, if I had one, I would be holding it.

The Gorba rolled his eyes. "On the station, you can get anything. But those are the drink specials listed over there by the bar."

Goggins took a look at the list.

The Gorba looked at me. "I take it you're not having anything."

"Correct," I said.

"Great," he replied flatly.

Goggins tapped his lips with a finger as he decided what cocktail to order. The Gorba was ready to leave when Goggins announced, "I'll have the piccala. It sounds delightful."

"Okay, bud. One piccala coming your way," the Gorba said as he typed the order in his comm device. "You haven't been here before, eh? At the station?"

"No," I said.

The Gorba laughed. "Not a talkative bot, are you?"

I didn't reply. It seemed superfluous.

Goggins smiled. "No, it's the strong and silent kind, but it is a pilot."

"Really?"

"Yes. In fact, we're interested in conversing with another pilot. A pilot who's been around the Edge for a while. A pilot who's familiar with the unchartered quadrants." Goggins leaned into the Gorba, "Know anyone like that?"

Down from the ceiling dropped a small serving tray with the piccala drink. It startled Goggins. "Thank you," he shouted up to the ceiling, not knowing if anyone was up there or not.

The Gorba laughed and pointed all around at the rough and tumble pilot patrons. "Take your pick." He had begun to walk away when I lay my hand on his shoulder and stopped him.

"I'd really appreciate your recommendation," I said. The weight of my hand pulled his shoulder down.

The Gorba yanked away. "I guess when you want something bad enough, you do speak. Okay, okay." He scanned the room again until his eyes locked onto a shadowy figure in the corner of the bar, drinking with a female android. "Him, over there. Been on the Edge for even longer than me."

Goggins and I strained to get a good look at the pilot in the corner. I focused my eyes and fine-tuned my vision. I snapped a pic of his face and ran it through my alien database to see if I could get a match on his species. I got a hit. His facial features matched the humanoid Degas race from the planet Degasia.

"Thank you, Mr. —" I started.

"Vetree," said the Gorba. "No mister, just call me Vetree."

"And what is his name?" I asked, nodding to the pilot in the corner.

"Him? He's Stoller. He served in the Degasian space force. Kicked out a few years ago. He's seen some action."

"Thank you, Vetree," said Goggins. Then he swallowed too much of his piccala and coughed it up all over my chest.

I looked down on him.

"Sorry, Gabe. Sorry." He tried to mop up my chest with a cocktail napkin. "My bad."

I gently pushed his arm away. "It's fine. Please stop."

"Okay," said Goggins as he peered again into the corner. "He's gone."

I looked over. Stoller wasn't sitting in the corner anymore. I scanned the bar. I spotted him heading out and had stood up to go after him when I saw Zara walk through the door. And Stoller saw her too.

Goggins pulled my arm down. "Sit. I think Zara may lead our pilot to us. She has her own ancient powers," he whispered. Goggins then stood up and waved. "Zara, Zara, we're over here."

Stoller watched Zara pass him. She glanced at Stoller as well. They'd locked eyes when she heard Goggins shout. She gave a slight smile to Stoller, turned and nodded to Goggins. She headed straight toward us. Stoller watched her walk to our table, then turned around and strolled back to the bar, where he kept an eye on us. I guessed he'd changed his mind about leaving.

Goggins kept waving at Zara even though she'd acknowledged him. "Geez, Goggins. I see you. I see you. Way to be inconspicuous," she said as she took a seat.

Goggins smiled. Mission accomplished. Stoller had stayed in the bar.

Vetree hustled over to our table. "May I get you something?" he asked with more politeness in his voice than what we encountered earlier.

Without hesitation, Zara said, "Do you have Suissey gin?"

"Yes, absolutely. A crate was found floating in space just yesterday. I'll get that to you right away," said Vetree with a toothy smile.

Zara smiled back. I never saw her smile like that. "How convenient. Thank you," she said. Vetree typed in her order and backed away, bumping into a table as he continued staring at Zara.

"Found floating in space? More like pirated in space," Goggins said in a hushed tone. He turned to Zara, "I think you have an admirer."

"What, the waiter?" she said.

"No, the pilot over there." He pointed to the bar. Zara turned slowly and locked eyes again with Stoller. He raised his glass to her. She smiled and turned back to us.

Zara's Suissey gin lowered down to our table. "I can't stand the Suissey, but they make good gin. And if it was pirated, it makes it taste all the better." She swigged the shot and gave a satisfied sigh. "Who is he?" asked Zara, nodding to the pilot watching her.

"His name is Stoller. Former military pilot," I offered. "He's a Degasian."

"I heard of them. He's handsome," she said.

"I bet he thinks the same of you," said Goggins.

"I hope he has brains, too," she said.

"He must, to be a pilot," I said.

Goggins and Zara gave me a look like I was bragging. "What? A certain amount of brain or CPU power, memorization, math and spatial organization is needed. That's just a fact," I explained.

Zara laughed and put her hand on my hand. "Kidding. We know."

Then I felt stupid.

Vetree passed by. "Would you like another, miss?"

"No thank you. One's my limit," she said.

"Don't worry about the cost. The pilot at the bar bought that last round for you," he said.

Zara and Goggins' eyebrows shot up.

"Mine too?" asked Goggins.

"No," said Vetree as he walked away.

"It's normally polite to invite the buyer of a cocktail over to your table," whispered Goggins.

"Only if you want to," said Zara.

"Do you want to find Synthia or not?" asked Goggins.

Zara didn't even turn around to the bar to face Stoller—she just waved her hand over like she was flagging him down. She pointed at the empty seat next to her.

Stoller smiled at Zara's wave, paid his bill, swaggered over and sat at our table. His skin was gray-green, and his eyes were brown. He was tall and trim. His age was hard to decipher. My alien database said that the Degasians could age upwards of one hundred and fifty years. A safe bet would be that he was seventy-five which made him not young and not old.

Stoller drank his Charbeaux beer and looked at me and Goggins. Probably summing us up, trying to understand our relationship to each other. That reminded me of a joke Dr. Damiel Kell told me. *Have you heard the one about a robot, Heragi and Estarian who walk into a bar...*

"I'm Dr. Goggins."

"Stoller," said the Degasian.

"This is Gabe. And this is Zara, who also has a doctorate," Goggins continued.

Stoller nodded at me and then turned to Zara. He raised his

beer to her. "Pleasure to meet you," he said with a smile that, I had to admit, was appealing.

Zara raised her empty shot glass. "Thank you for the shot."

"Looks like you need another," he said.

Zara shook her head. "I'm good."

Stoller raised his hands like he wasn't going to argue with her. "What brings you to the station?" he asked instead.

"We're traveling through and need help finding a friend," she said.

"Maybe they don't want to be found. Lots of folks like that on Charbeaux Station." He smiled and took another swig.

"Truth is — she was taken," said Zara.

"Zara, please," Goggins chastised her for telling the truth.

Stoller held up his hand to Goggins to stop him from speaking down to Zara. "Hey, don't worry. This is the Edge. Everyone is here because something went sideways in their life one way or another, or they are just born loners."

"We don't want this repeated to anyone," warned Goggins.

"Hard to keep secrets on the station. All these folks have done good and done bad. Nothing shocks anyone, and everyone keeps their mouth shut for the most part. The best advice is to not have secrets. That way, you can't be betrayed." Stoller turned and studied me before staring at the bottom of his empty glass. He waved to Vetree to get him another beer. Vetree nodded.

Goggins shifted in his seat. I bio-scanned his vitals, and they were rising. He felt a threat from Stoller, and he wasn't wrong.

Stoller's next beer lowered from the ceiling. He grabbed it and leaned forward, spilling Goggins' drink. He grabbed it just before it fell over. Goggins drank what remained of his piccala and suppressed a cough. I hoped he wouldn't spew on my chest again. I turned slightly. Goggins held it down.

"Zara, tell him what you found in the satellite comm logs," I said.

She pulled out her coder and reviewed the findings. "I found a comm string from Heragi to a ship in this vicinity. There were two messages. Encrypted. I picked up on three words that I'm not familiar with — *karakova, mawzi,* and *salutia.*"

"Does that mean anything to you?" asked Goggins.

Stoller's eyes turned downward. His finger circled the rim of his beer glass. His head swung to one side. "Yeah, that means something to me. It means I better get going." He stood.

Zara jerked on his sleeve. He let her pull him down. His face came close to hers. She let go of his arm. He swept his head down and then pulled it up to look at us. There was a bleakness in his expression. I monitored his vitals and compared them against the baseline for his race. They were diving downward which told me he was unsettled, probably thinking of memories that weren't pleasant.

"Please," whispered Zara.

He sighed. "*Karakova* is the Karakova Highway. It's not documented anywhere like all the space highways in chartered galaxy territories. You can find it if you've traveled on it before and keep track of the nearby planets and their seasonal rotations. If you get on the wrong highway out in the uncharted quadrants, it can take you months to figure it out, and you could run out of food, water — then you're in big trouble."

"I never heard of it," said Goggins.

"There'll be a lot of things you never heard of in the Edge. And some things you learn that you wish you didn't know," Stoller said before he drank half his beer.

"And *Mawzi?*" I asked.

"That's a planet. Has a thin atmosphere. It's cold. A barren planet but habitable underground," he said.

"And *Salutia?*" asked Zara.

"That's an old Edger term. Means good luck." Stoller turned to Zara. "Does that help?"

Zara nodded. "Yes, thank you."

"We'll need help finding the Karakova Highway," I said.

"That's tricky. I can tell you, but it's hit or miss. And you don't want to miss." He finished his beer and swirled the glass into the middle of the table which sprung beer suds onto Goggins' face.

"I wish I could help you more," Stoller said as he drunkenly looked over to Zara.

"You can," she said. "You can come with us."

Stoller laughed. None of us laughed.

He looked around the table. "I have things to do here," he countered.

Zara pulled out a gun and pressed it into his rib cage. "I don't care. I care about my friend."

Goggins' back straightened. Mine almost did too. I did not see that coming.

Stoller weighed his options. He smiled at her. "I hope your friend isn't your husband," he said as he pushed her gun away from his body.

"She's not," said Goggins. "Just an old lady. Well, *older,* I should say. Mature is a better term. She's sophisticated — a brilliant lady. Maybe a little bit out there."

"And what do I get in return?" asked Stoller as he settled back into his seat and lowered his gaze at us. "I mean, I'm sure being in your company is charming, but a pilot needs to be paid."

"You want galaxy credits? Name your price," said Zara as she held up her coder.

"Yes, I want credits. And I want some help myself."

"With what?" I asked.

"Retrieving a ship someone stole from me."

"Your ship was pirated? You're a pilot without a ship," said Goggins with a snort. I thought he was tipsy. I scanned his biometrics and confirmed it. Two drunks at the Blue Edger may not be uncommon, but I didn't like it at my table, at all.

Stoller frowned at Goggins. "Do you want my help or not?

Maybe I'll let you float for months on the wrong highway," he threatened.

I hit Goggins in the chest.

"Ow!" He rubbed his chest. "Don't hit me, Gabe, or I'll recode your CPU, you great big tin-bot."

"Yes, we want your help," I said.

"Where do you think your ship is?" asked Zara.

"Off the Karakova Highway. It's on a planet," Stoller answered.

"Who stole it?" I asked.

"Just a stupid kid."

"What's the kid's name?" I asked, trying to gain more detailed information.

"Tristan. Tristan Oliveria."

I scanned the name in my alien database. I got a hit.

Oliveria.

The Provence of Oliveria.

Some kid.

"Tristan Oliveria. Son of Swina Oliveria, ruler of the Oliveria Providence," I stated.

"He's a prince?" Goggins gulped.

"Technically, no. They're not royal. But, yes, he's sort of *princely*," replied Stoller as he shrugged.

"How did he steal it?" inquired Goggins.

"Ever play quinker?" asked Stoller, leaning in with a smile.

"You lost your ship in a card game?" said Zara. She folded her arms against her chest.

"He cheated." Stoller mimicked Zara's arm fold.

"How do you know he cheated?" asked Goggins.

"He — I just do! Where is Vetree when you need him?" His gaze searched the bar for the waiter.

"Hmm. Sounds like he's a better cheater than you," snapped Goggins.

Stoller sneered and leaned in closer to Goggins.

"Enough! We'll help you get your ship back," said Zara in a snap decision. She wanted Synthia back as soon as possible. I got it. Their bond was deep. I scanned her rising vital signs; she must be thinking of Synthia and was anxious to leave. It was time to wrap this up.

"Our ship is the *Alyssia*. Gate 6707. Be on board in two hours," I said, rising to leave. Goggins and Zara stood up.

"Two hours. The *Alyssia*. 6707. Got it," said Stoller with a nod.

I turned around and saw Stoller signal Vetree for another beer. I hoped he wasn't too drunk when he got to the *Alyssia*. The thought of wasting away for months on the wrong Edger highway wasn't appealing.

We headed back to our ship.

The Kell children would be arriving soon, and I was looking forward to hearing news from them. Specifically, any news on their mother, Ava, and if she still hated me.

3

───────

We received our weapons load at the gate, and I was supervising the load in when Feti came over my comms. "Gabe, the Kell children have arrived at the station. They're heading over to the *Alyssia* now."

"Thank you, Feti," I said. A feeling of warmth rose in my chest. It would be good to see them.

I signed off on the delivery-bot's order and was heading back to the bridge when a question hit me. "Feti?"

"Yes, Gabe?"

"Is there anyone else with the children?"

"Do you mean Damiel or Ava Kell?"

"Uh, yeah. That's what I mean," I sputtered.

"No, Gabe. They did not indicate that," it said. "Sorry."

"No need to be sorry. Or be sorry for me. Okay?" This was getting embarrassing. Feti would know I couldn't stop thinking of Ava. I'd better shut up.

"Okay, Gabe," said Feti. "The children have arrived. They're boarding our ramp."

I changed direction from the bridge to the ramp to greet

them. I saw a flash running closer to me. It was small and fast. Talia. She hugged me.

She pulled back her head and put her forehead against mine.

Talia was born deaf and had a chip inserted into her brain as a small child that linked to a transceiver on her arm comm that both spoke her words out loud and transmitted sounds to her brain. This was common for the deaf on Heragi and other planets in the galaxy.

What wasn't common – at all – was that her roboticist parents, Damiel and Ava Kell, discovered, she had an ancient DNA gene make-up that made telepathy possible. Telepathy and any of the ancient gifts were outlawed by the Heragi.

Talia's parents placed a sensor in her brain which enabled me to communicate directly with her on a thought link. When Talia's sensor was removed and placed in her sister's brain, Synthia was able to train Talia so that she was fully telepathic on her own.

And, on our last mission, with additional training from Synthia, I honed my telepathy skills and was able to share thoughts with Talia, Honora and Synthia – or anyone who had this ancient gift.

Talia sent me a thought. *Hello, Gabe. I missed you.*

Thank you. I missed you, too.

Alex was next in line, and he stuck out his hand for mine. I shook it. It didn't feel natural to me, but humans liked to shake hands.

"Thanks for letting us tag along," he said with a grin.

Honora was last and threw a heavy bag onto the floor. "How come I'm carrying all of our gear?" she complained. "Hey, Gabe. Surprise! Right?"

"I didn't expect your parents would let you out of their sight," I said.

"They didn't have much of a choice," said Honora.

"Explanation, please."

"You're not going to like this," said Alex.

"My judgement system for adolescents' behavior isn't very high. And your parents are the ones who programmed it that way," I said, trying to alleviate them of any worry.

Talia held up her arm comm for others to hear. "We ran away."

My head jerked back in surprise. I regained my composure. These kids.

I shook my head and stared down at the Kell children. They gazed downward, trying not to make eye contact. I reached out to Talia and turned her chin upward, so she looked into my eyes.

Talia sent me a thought. *Don't be mad.*

"I'm not mad," I said out loud. "But I am concerned. Think of your parents. They'll be upset."

"They know we're meeting up with you to find Synthia, but they don't know exactly *where* we are since I hacked our navigation beacon, so they can't track us." Honora smirked.

"And whose spaceship did you take? Or should I say *steal*?"

"Just a small planet jumper. Don't worry—we're having it shuttled back to Zaradorba on a shuttle that can't be traced back to us here," said Honora.

"With Honora's new pilot skills, getting here was a piece of cake," said Alex.

Alex high-fived Honora.

"Children, this is not good. Your parents will be worried. You must go back," I said.

"Our parents can't protect us anymore," said Alex.

"That was the whole point of the initial mission they gave me. To protect you and deliver you to Zaradorba. Yes, we did make some side trips, but I got you there, eventually," I said.

"We helped too, you know," said Honora.

"Yes, you did. I'm not discounting that. All of your skills are valuable. So valuable that the Heragi Empire will do anything to capture you. That is why your parents want you to be safe on

Zaradorba. Where they can have your Uncle Jeb's rebels protect you," I said.

"Our skills, you said. Don't you mean our DNA?" asked Alex.

"Yes, that too," I said.

"There's something we found out after you left," said Honora.

"What?"

"General Foxwell's special agent Jakawa took DNA samples from me and Talia when he captured us on Korfu while we were rescuing our parents from prison," explained Honora. "And he gave those samples to Stefano."

I thought about what Honora said, and negative scenarios streamed into my CPU. It was not surprising that Jakawa took samples but finding out about this now made me think of what Stefano could be doing with Synthia.

"If they have Talia's telepathy DNA or Alex's telekinesis DNA or your enhanced DNA, Honora, it won't take them long to manipulate it and then encode it into their subjects," I said. "And with Synthia's telepathy and mind splitting ability, they may be able to do this all very quickly."

The children were quiet. Alex and Talia glanced back to Honora.

I looked at her too. "Honora, did you erase my code that you uploaded into your sensor on our last mission?" I asked. She had promised to get rid of all my rogue code that she had taken without my permission when she wanted to study my pilot programs that her parents had coded into my system.

It wasn't that a pilot or combat program was so special coded into a robot. But the programs became so when we uploaded them to Talia's old sensor that she didn't need anymore and placed it in Honora. Then those programs attached to Honora's DNA strands and made her an enhanced human.

But Honora had earlier downloaded all my programs and rogue code — all of it was uploaded to Honora's DNA.

I hoped the answer to my question was yes.

"No," Honora said as she looked into my eyes. "I meant to, but then we rescued Mom and Dad, and then General Foxwell took us." She leaned against the wall and lowered her head. "And then it was too late."

Oh, no. No. No. No.

A pain hit my chest. I stifled a groan.

"Do your parents know?" I asked, hardly ready for the answer.

"Yes," said Alex.

Now Ava was going to hate me even more. The pain in my chest became stronger.

"What did they say?" I asked.

"After Mom stopped crying, she said we were basically grounded on Zaradorba for the rest of our lives," said Honora.

Talia's transceiver played, "Mom and Dad talked with Uncle Jeb. And then he left on his ship. We don't know where he went."

"It's really unfair that they grounded all of us, since it was Honora who didn't erase your code on her sensor," said Alex as he gave Honora a look.

"Do you know why your mother cried?" I asked.

The children were silent.

"It's because of Honora's DNA that was intertwined with my coding. The coding that made me sentient and that makes me able to kill humans or anyone without discretion, which is against Heragi law. My rogue code is intertwined with your ancient DNA strains," I explained.

Honora put her head into her hands. Talia went to comfort her sister. Alex put his hand on Honora's shoulder for support.

"You see, now the Heragi Empire can create rogue cyborgs with your ancient powers. They can do this to any humanoid's

DNA. They can create an army of cyborgs. And they will have advanced piloting and combat skills, all of your ancient gifts, with increased humanoid strength. They'll be able to take over their brains, their will and order them to do anything they want — all to enhance Heragi Empire control," I concluded.

"Okay, I get it. I'm sorry. But we're here, Gabe. We're here to help," said Honora with more concern in her voice than I'd heard since I met her.

"Get settled and meet back on the bridge. We're leaving soon." I must have stressed her nervous system enough with that explanation. She didn't need any more guilt laid on her.

The children went to their quarters, and I turned around and headed toward the bridge.

Zara and Goggins were at their stations, conducting prep work for our trip.

I plopped into my commander seat with a heaviness I didn't want to hide. It made Zara and Goggins jump.

"What's up? The kids are okay?" Zara was trying to read my mood.

"Yeah. They'll be on the bridge shortly," I replied

"Nice of them to help find Synthia. They're good kids," Goggins said.

I swung around to him. "Honora didn't erase my code. Jakawa took blood samples and Stefano has them. The children stole a spaceship and ran away to get here."

"They're rotten kids. Just rotten," Goggins spit out.

We were all silent for a bit.

I reviewed the pilot console to keep busy.

"No, they're *not* rotten. We all know that. They're good kids. It's just that *they are kids*," said Zara.

"With superhuman powers. Sorry — *ancient* powers." Goggins made air quotes when he said *ancient*.

"They need more training. They need Synthia now more than ever," Zara said. She went back to her coding.

Feti came over the ship's comm system. "Gabe, we have another visitor. A man named Stoller is requesting permission to board."

"Allow him entrance, Feti. Thank you. Mr. Stoller will be joining us for part of our voyage," I explained.

"Very well," said Feti.

Alex, Honora and Talia entered the bridge, said hello to Zara and Goggins and took their seats. Then Talia's cicichimp ran down the hallway and jumped on Talia's shoulder.

"That reminds me. Look, Talia. See what I got you on the station?" Goggins pulled out the fake cicichimp and showed Talia, who smiled.

She raised her arm comm. "Thank you, Dr. Goggins."

Goggins gave Talia the cicichimp doll. She hugged it. Then the real cicichimp's eyes narrowed, and it grabbed the doll and ran off the bridge. Talia jumped up.

Then we all heard a scuffle in the hall leading to the bridge. I turned around to find Stoller walking in with the cicichimp animatronic in his hands and the real cicichimp sitting on his shoulder.

Talia laughed along with the other kids.

"Someone lose a cicichimp? I've got two here," said Stoller with a grin. "Ah, I bet these belong to you. Am I right?" Stoller bent down and gave them both to Talia. She grabbed them and said thank you via her transceiver. Stoller nodded.

"Aren't you going to introduce me?" Stoller asked as he pointed to the children. "Are we dropping them off at some boarding school?"

The kids looked at each other.

"Who are we? Who are you?" asked Alex as he raised his hands toward the cicichimp doll. It floated out of Talia's arms and across the bridge into Alex's hand.

"Hey, don't do that," yelled Talia through her arm comm She jumped up and grabbed her cicichimp doll back.

"Sorry, Talia" said Alex as he sulked back into his seat.

Stoller had a surprised look on this face. "Whoa. That was a neat trick, kid. How'd you do it?"

"It wasn't a trick," said Zara. "These kids are — special."

"Special?" Stoller nestled into a seat. "What else can they do?"

"Don't be surprised if one of these kids saves your life," said Zara.

"Or maybe we won't," said Honora as she buckled up.

He threw up his hands. "Okay, okay. Pardon my grouchiness. I surrender."

"Stoller, this is Alex, Honora and Talia Kell," I said. Stoller nodded to each one of them. "And this is Stoller."

"And why is *he* on the ship?" asked Honora.

"He's going to help us pilot through the unchartered quadrants. Help us find the planet that Synthia is on," I explained.

"And in exchange, you help me retrieve my ship in the Oliveria Providence. Shouldn't be hard," said Stoller.

"Retrieving Synthia may be hard," said Alex. "Are you up for that?"

"I'm not coming with you to Mawzi. I'm just pointing you in the right direction," said Stoller as he pushed his hat over his eyes to catch some sleep.

Zara kicked his boot. Stoller jumped up. "What the heck? I'm getting a bit tired of being hit by this team."

"What do you mean you're just here to *point us in the right direction*? Part of the deal is you helping us retrieve Synthia," said Zara. "We'll get your ship *after* we get Synthia."

"I don't see that written in my contract," said Stoller, standing up.

"What contract?" asked Alex.

"Exactly, kid," said Stoller. "Listen, I'll help you find your little friend. But don't you think it would be a better fight if you had my ship and the *Alyssia*? Two is better than one, no?"

Everyone was silent. He had a point.

"We'll get your ship first," I said.

"Easy for you to play with Synthia's life or rebel lives that they may be forcing her to out," said Zara with venom.

"It's not an easy decision, but it's the right decision," I said.

Time was what Zara was concerned about, but that needed to be balanced with the likelihood of winning.

"I agree. We need every advantage when fighting. But we do need to retrieve our new shipmate's ship as quick as we can. Okay?" said Alex with a maturity I hadn't heard before in his voice.

Zara turned back to her coder. "Fine. Let's make it quick."

I was getting tired of this conversation. I'd better lift off before Stoller changed his mind.

"Feti, begin launch procedures," I said.

"Thanks, kid. Thanks, Mr. Robot," said Stoller.

"His name is Gabe," said Talia's transceiver.

Feti began launch procedures.

"Got it," said Stoller as he glanced at Talia.

"Lifting off," I said as we cruised out of the Charbeaux Station. The quick launch whipped everyone back into their chair.

"Oof," cried Stoller as he gripped his seat. For a pilot, he seemed a bit rusty to space travel or at least lift off. In a few seconds, our flight stabilized, and everyone unbuckled from their seats. We were entering deep space.

"We need the coordinates to get us to Mawzi," said Goggins. "Do you mind typing them into my navigation device?" He handed Stoller a tablet.

"Sure." Stoller looked over to Zara, who smiled at him.

"I should thank you ahead of time. The woman we are retrieving means the world to me," she said.

Stoller took the navigation pad and typed in coordinates. He handed it back to Goggins.

Stoller looked at her, rolled his eyes and said, "My pleasure, Zara."

"Hey, you were the one who turned around at the door in the bar," she said.

"You looked familiar. Like my sister," he said.

"Really?" said Goggins. "Now I've heard every line in the galaxy. Gee, can I meet your sister?"

"Nope, she's dead."

"That's a conversation killer," said Goggins.

Talia lifted her arm comm "He's lying. He doesn't have a sister."

"Where did you find these kids?" asked Stoller.

Zara snapped, "Nice. Lying already. I hope you are truthful about the coordinates to Mawzi."

"No, those are legit. I just didn't want to say that your stunning beauty is the reason I turned around at the bar." Stoller addressed Talia. "Does that check out, kid?"

Talia nodded.

"See?" said Stoller.

"Good save," said Goggins as he typed in the coordinates to Mawzi.

"Feti, please make a new navigation plan. Dr. Goggins is uploading the coordinates right now," I said.

"Affirmative, Gabe," said Feti.

Feti turned our ship, and we were moving swiftly toward Mawzi.

"Feti? When will we arrive at Mawzi?" I asked.

"That will be two solar days, Gabe. I will alert you when we are nearing the solar system for that planet," it said.

"Thank you." I turned the chair around. "Everyone. This is an important mission and a dangerous one. We all need to get along to the best of our ability. Do I have everyone's agreement?"

I looked at each one of the team members.

Everyone nodded and agreed.

"Okay, good. Now why don't you all have some dinner in the galley? I'm sure Feti will make something for each one of you that will satisfy your taste buds."

They all got up and left the bridge.

Finally.

This group better operate as a team before we got to Mawzi or this mission would not go well.

Perhaps Feti should feed them wine. On second thought, that wouldn't work with the children. There had to be another way to bond the team.

"Gabe, we have a ship on our port side moving fast. They just turned on their weapons system," alerted Feti.

"What?" I checked my monitors. It had crept up from nowhere.

Nothing bonds a crew more than a battle.

I got on the ship's comm and called everyone back to the bridge.

4

———

The crew ran to the bridge and stared at the unknown spaceship off our port.

"Feti, can you get an identifier on that ship?" I asked.

"I've been trying, Gabe, but it appears to be a ghost ship," said Feti.

"A ghost ship?" asked Talia through her transceiver.

"It's a ship with no unique identifier. None that we can pick up on," answered Alex.

"They fired up their weapons system," I said.

"What are they? Pirates?" asked Zara.

"What do they want? Galaxy credits? Our missile supplies? Us?" asked Goggins as he ran his fingers through his hair.

"No, no and no," said Stoller. "They're not pirates. They're bounty hunters. Or I should say the captain is a bounty hunter."

"You're familiar with this ship?" asked Goggins.

"Yes," Stoller said.

"Do we have a bounty on us?" asked Zara.

"We may," I said.

Stoller rubbed his stubbly chin.

Zara took Stoller's shoulder and whipped him around to face her. "Do you have a bounty on *your* head?"

"Um," Stoller said. He glanced at Talia. He knew he couldn't lie. "Maybe, yeah. I mean yes. An old one."

Goggins hit his console. "Geez, are you kidding me? And you didn't think that was important to tell us?"

"Your interview process wasn't exactly thorough. You wanted a pilot to get you through the uncharted quadrants." Stoller spread out his arms. "And you got one."

"Alex, take the port gun turret," I said.

"Copy that," said Alex as he ran off the bridge.

"Take a seat, Stoller." I pointed to the co-commander chair. "Everyone, buckle up."

"Who's the bounty hunter?" asked Zara.

"His name is Kaleb Kron. He's actually pretty good at quinker, but I'm better." He smirked.

"We don't care if he's good at quinker. Tell us about his ship," snapped Zara.

"It's called the *Legessy*. It's got four gun turrets and two missile systems. One for long range, and one for short range. And two escape pods. It's fast and agile. It has a jammer that throws off any tracking of their movements. That's how it snuck up on us."

"Honora, work on hacking into their missile system," yelled Zara.

"On it," said Honora as she pulled out her coder.

"I'll work on getting into their navigation system." Zara leaned over her console.

Feti came over the ship's comm. "Gabe, the captain of the *Legessy* would like to talk with you. He's requesting video and audio transmission."

I looked over to Stoller who was shaking his head.

"Granted," I said.

"What did you do that for?" Stoller whispered.

I didn't answer him because I didn't have a good answer. I just wanted to annoy him.

A hologram image appeared from our comm system at the front of the bridge.

"My name is Kaleb Kron. I believe you have a wanted bail skipper on board your ship," he said.

I scanned his face and ran his voice through my alien directory which hit a match. He was a Lubian. An alien species with a crowded planet whose biggest trade was mining a specialized lightweight but strong ore used in spaceship construction. Undoubtedly, that was what the *Legessy* was made from.

Kaleb was missing one of his ears. In fact, his whole left side was melted. Must have been a bounty that went bad.

"My name is Gabe, commander of the *Alyssia*," I said.

"I thought it would be odd to find Mr. Gates this far out in the Edge. Well, that is neither here nor there. You have James Stoller on board. He is wanted on spaceship theft. I don't know how you handle law and order on Heragi, but here in the Edge, we need to help nearby planets with their criminal containment."

"Ship? What ship did you steal?" whispered Zara to Stoller.

I muted our comms to Kron.

"My ship," said Stoller. "But I didn't steal it. I won it in a quinker game."

"The one that Prince Tristan won?" whispered Goggins.

I was getting confused. "You mean you won it in a quinker game and then lost it later in a quinker game?"

"Exactly," said Stoller.

"I think you should stop playing quinker," said Zara.

"Kaleb Kron knows I won my ship fair and square. It's just that I won it from a guy with a huge ego and a fancy family," said Stoller, his voice rising.

"Another prince?" asked Goggins.

"No, *none* of them are princes," said Stoller, shaking his finger toward Goggins.

"Quiet," I yelled. I had had enough.

I unmuted our comms.

"Kaleb, I'm afraid I can't accommodate you. We need Stoller for a brief engagement, and then he will be on his own, and you can keep pursuing him then," I explained.

"What the—" said Stoller under his breath. He stepped up in front of our hologram screen camera.

"Kaleb, hey there. Long time no see. What Gabe means is you're out of luck today. And I believe you are out of your jurisdiction as we just crossed over into the fourth Ulysses quadrant. And unless I'm mistaken, there are no extradition treaties that the Ulysses government has signed." Stoller gave a curt laugh and sat down. He was very proud of himself for his lawyerly statement.

A smile grew over Kaleb's face. He pointed to the side — to a crew member. The hologram went black. Not good.

Who was Stoller, and why did we have to choose him in the Blue Edger bar?

Feti came on the comm system. "Two missiles have been launched from the *Legessy*."

In two successive hits, the missiles slammed into our port side. We were tossed right, then left. Sparks flew from the system monitors located on the port side.

I looked around to Talia and Honora who were now holding hands but weren't hurt. I saw that Talia was frightened. I sent her a thought. *I won't let anyone hurt you.*

I know, she thought back.

Alex flashed in my mind. He was in the port side turret.

"Alex? Are you okay?" I yelled into our internal comms.

No answer.

I'd started to get up when Stoller yelled, "Get us out of here. I'll check on the kid."

"Fire up our missile system, Feti," I ordered.

"It's ready, Gabe."

I began firing missiles at the *Legessy*. The ship was smaller than the *Alyssia*, but Edward Gates, the proprietor of our ship, had previously installed a first-rate missile system and, better yet, a super-g drive system. I reviewed fight or flight calculations in my mind.

The *Legessy* spun around to our starboard side.

"Gabe, Kaleb is on the move," yelled Goggins.

"I see him." I maneuvered the *Alyssia* for us to get the advantage angle.

Honora unbuckled herself and headed off the bridge. "I'll take the starboard turret."

"Wait!" yelled Zara.

"No, she's okay. She has all my combat programs encoded in her. She'll know how to operate it," I reminded Zara.

A buzz sounded on Zara's coder. She looked down and smiled. "That girl. Blasted, she's good. She just sent me her code for their weapons system. She almost got it."

"Gabe, why don't we just punch out of here? We could outrun him," said Goggins as he wiped his sweaty brow.

"We may outrun him for a while, but I'm not sure he couldn't keep up, and I don't want him to follow us. We need to hurt him," I said.

"But not kill him, right?" asked Goggins.

"No, Dr. Goggins. Just damage his ship. I don't kill indiscriminately, if you're asking me," I said.

"Just checking," said Goggins.

"Unless it gets real bad," I added.

"That makes total sense," Goggins said in his snarky tone with another wipe to his forehead.

I was able to get off one missile that nicked the *Legessy*'s hull. I turned back toward Talia. She had her eyes closed. She was deep in meditation.

Alex is okay, was the thought she sent me.

I nodded and continued evasive maneuvers as we fired on the

Legessy. On my console, it calculated the rounds of gunfire that Honora had been releasing. She was doing some serious damage to Kaleb's ship. His radio tower got knocked down. Good shot.

Stoller was on the comm. "Alex is all right but a bit knocked up. I'll take over the port turret. Honora's doing very good on the starboard side, by the way."

I laughed out loud. But it sounded like a succession of grunts.

"Was that a laugh?" asked Zara as she looked up.

"I think it was," said Goggins.

We took a hard hit on our port side. It was a direct hit on our turret. Alex's voice came over the comm. "Stoller's hurt. It's pretty bad."

"I'm in," shouted Zara. "Turning off Kaleb's weapons system. Ha!"

I flew us right under the *Legessy*'s hull and fired six missiles directly up into its aft and stern. That should knock him out for a while. The *Legessy* wasn't expecting the agility of the *Alyssia*. It had no chance on that last move. The missiles made its stern inoperable. It drifted off into space.

"Okay, now we can leave. Hold on!" I shouted over the comm. I threw our super-g engine into force. We were all pushed back into our seats.

"Ahh," Goggins cried.

It would only last five seconds, then we'd lower out of the super-g.

One. Two. Three. Four. Five.

The g-force subsided. We slowed. I took us down to cruising speed.

"Gabe, warn us next time," complained Goggins. "I've got a splitting headache." He grabbed his head.

Talia handed Goggins the fake cicichimp doll. He put it between the console and his head. "Ah, that's better. Thank you, Talia."

Talia smiled and hugged her real cicichimp, who chirped at Goggins.

We had traveled some fifty thousand miles in five seconds. I had no idea where we were or if I had taken us far off course from entering the Karakova Highway.

If Stoller was badly injured and by badly, I meant dead, then I wasn't sure we would know how to get back. I hoped he wasn't dead. I wanted to ask him more about his quinker card game. Oddly, I was starting to like him.

"I'll check on everyone in the back," I said, trying to remain calm in front of the crew.

I got up and marched back to the turret to see Stoller.

The smell of burning flesh hit my sensors before I could see Stoller's arm. To be exact, his right arm that was now severed at the elbow. His hand sat lifeless on the ground nearby. He groaned in pain. The wound didn't look fatal, just temporarily debilitating. Alex had already wrapped up a tourniquet on Stoller's arm to stop the bleeding.

"Ah, Kaleb. An eye for an eye, huh? Or should I say an arm for an ear? Not a fair trade in my view." Stoller cursed out the bounty hunter. "Sorry, kids." He grimaced in pain.

I looked over to Alex. He had a bloody cut over his right eyebrow. "Are you okay?"

"Yeah." He wiped some blood out of his eyes.

"Hey, what about me, big boy?" joked Stoller.

I bent down to look at his arm. "We can laser the wound, but the medbay doesn't have a full regenerative grafting machine onboard."

"Just my luck," replied Stoller.

Honora walked over and looked down at Stoller. "Gabe, let

me in," she said. I backed up and let her get closer to the injured man.

"Hey, kid, you looked pretty comfortable shooting that gun. Where did you learn to do that?" he asked between grimaces.

Honora tapped the side of her head with a finger. "It's all in here."

Stoller nodded, but I could tell he didn't exactly know what she meant.

Honora looked at his arm and then looked him in the eyes. "I can help you," she said.

"What? Bandage me up? Okay, let's get some pain meds too, huh?"

Honora looked up to me. "Gabe, let's get him to the medbay."

I picked up Stoller.

"Whoa. Ah…" He grimaced in pain.

I carried him down the hall and into the medbay. Honora and Alex followed. I put Stoller down on the center surgery bed. Alex had picked up Stoller's severed arm, and he laid it on the bed next to where it once was attached.

Goggins and Zara followed us into the room.

Zara went up to Stoller. She put her hand on his forehead. "I'm sorry," she said softly.

"That's what I get for being a sucker for beauty," he said with a laugh. "If you really want to help me, find me some pain meds."

Zara smiled and ran to the med cabinet. She grabbed a pain relief injector and returned to the table. Just before she was about to shoot Stoller with the shot, Honora grabbed Zara's hand to stop her. "Wait."

"What? No, don't wait," pleaded Stoller.

Honora shook her head.

"It will be okay," Zara said as she stepped back.

Honora walked up to Stoller's severed arm. Stoller looked

around the room and couldn't understand why everyone was letting Honora look over him with no urgency. He was starting to lose more blood, and he knew he only had a few minutes.

With his good arm, Stoller reached out to Zara. "Help me."

She returned to him and took his hand. "She will help you."

Stoller looked back toward Honora who had undone his tourniquet, picked up his severed arm and joined it to his shredded arm. She pushed them together.

Stoller stifled a scream.

Honora then put both her palms down on the conjoined area. She closed her eyes tight. Her mouth opened and her head went backwards. A light began to emanate from the severed area of Stoller's arm.

I again smelled burning flesh. I stepped forward to look closer. She wasn't burning flesh away; she was fusing flesh and bone together. Honora was healing him.

Stoller's face became calm. I scanned his bio-metrics. The pain was subsiding, and his nervous system and vitals were normalizing. He looked down at this arm and couldn't believe what he saw — two pieces becoming one. He looked back up to Honora who brought her head forward. Her mouth closed. The light subsided from her palms. She pulled her hands away.

Honora staggered backwards, and I caught her. I lifted her to a nearby bed. She sent me a thought. *I'm so tired.*

Rest. You did good, Honora.

She smiled and closed her eyes to rest. Talia grabbed her hand and kissed it. Alex touched Stoller's arm. "How does it feel?"

Stoller picked it up and moved it. He flattened out his fingers and then flexed his arm. He made a fist and then relaxed his hand.

"I can't believe it. How did she do that? Who is she? What is she?" he asked, baffled.

"She's my sister," Alex said. He headed back to Honora and kissed her forehead. "She's a healer."

Stoller looked over to Honora. "Thank you, kid."

Zara looked at his arm and laughed.

Goggins also examined Stoller's arm. "You'll be back to playing cards in no time!"

Stoller laughed. "Yes, you're right. Care for a game?"

"Sure, why not?" said Goggins.

"And you, Zara?" asked Stoller.

"Count me in," she said.

And there it was. A battle. A bonding. A team.

I looked over to Honora being comforted by her sister and brother. But it was more than that. We all witnessed a healing. And I was sure that would bond us forever, more than any battle.

5

I was working with Zara and Goggins on trying to understand our current placement in the deep space quadrant when Stoller came up to us. He was showered and cleaned up. It must have done him some good since he seemed at peace, at least temporarily.

"I had to punch us into super-g to get some miles between us and Kaleb," I explained to him.

He plopped in a chair behind me. "No, that was good. You had to do it," said Stoller. "Um, I want to apologize for not telling you guys about the bounty. I didn't think you would get dragged into it."

"Is there anything else we should know about?" asked Goggins.

"Probably. Can you narrow that question a bit?" said Stoller with a chuckle.

"Are there any other bounty hunters, former colleagues, galaxy police or irate aliens, humanoids or androids that could be hunting you down?" asked Zara as she put down her coder.

Stoller rubbed his wet hair and thought. "Yeah. Definitely," he said with a wide smile.

"Geez," said Goggins as he laid his head down on the cici-chimp doll again.

"What?" said Stoller. "What do you want? If you come to the Edge, it's for a reason that probably involves some unhappy former parties you associated with. And if you stay alive out in the Edge for any length of time, then you're bound to piss off said parties."

"It would have been nice to know about that," said Zara.

"Now you know," he said. "But does it help you at all? No, it doesn't."

"It will help us prepare," said Zara.

"You should always be prepared in the Edge," he said. "In a way, that was a helpful little run-in for us. Call it our *shake-out cruise*. Shake out all the bugs." He laughed in a way that made it hard to dislike him.

Goggins lifted his head and nodded. "We did show that Kaleb Kron the what-for. Wouldn't you agree Zara?"

Zara sighed. "Between Gabe's flying, Alex's target shooting, and Honora's coding, we did okay," she said.

Zara's comment made Stoller laugh even louder. "I'll take okay."

I didn't laugh out loud, but I was enjoying the banter and the warm feeling that started in my chest.

"Stoller, where are we?" I asked, turning my chair to him.

He took the co-commander seat and stared out the bridge window. He looked left and then he looked right.

"Slowly give me a three-sixty, so I can get my bearings," he asked politely.

I slowly turned the *Alyssia* on its axis a full three hundred and sixty degrees. When we reached our starting point, he swirled his finger in the air.

He pointed to a planet in the distance. "There! There it is!" He smiled. "Ah, you beauty. You were hiding from me, but I found you."

"What are you pointing at?" asked Goggins as he strained to look out the window and then to his navigation screen.

"That planet. Do you see it? That orange planet? You can just make out its rings," he said, pointing.

"Yes, I see it," I said.

"Got it," said Zara as she peered over Stoller's shoulder.

"Yep, I got it on my screen now," said Goggins.

"That, ladies and gentleman — and robots — is Lady Hypatia," he said.

"Really? The planet's name is Lady Hypatia?" There was doubt in Zara's voice.

"No. But that is what I call her," he said with a smile. He looked almost lovingly toward the planet.

"I didn't know planets were male or female," said Zara.

"They're not," said Goggins.

"I disagree, Doc," said Stoller. "She's a beauty." He turned and smiled at me. "Don't you agree, Gabe?"

I looked at the planet harder. *Perhaps I'm missing something*, I thought. The dozens of rings around it were unique.

"There is an aesthetic appeal," I offered.

Stoller smiled. "Exactly. She's gorgeous is what I think you mean."

Zara bit her lip. "So what is *her* significance?"

Stoller turned his seat around to face Zara. "Lady Hypatia is the key planet of the Karakova Highway. If you can find her, then you just need to head toward her, and then you can go multiple directions and levels on the highway," he explained.

"But what if we couldn't find her. Isn't that kind of random?" Zara asked.

Stoller nodded. "Yep, exactly. You got it. That's why I give her such reverence. When I find her, I fall in love with her all over again." He turned back toward the window.

Zara rolled her eyes. "As long as we found her," she whispered.

"Dr. Goggins, what's your calculation on when we would reach, um, *her*?" I asked.

Goggins was working on the navigational program. He looked up. "One day," he answered.

"That super-g saved us a few days' travel time," commented Stoller.

"Let's do it again," said Zara.

"We can't. The super-g isn't as accurate as one would think. We could bypass it by tens of thousands of miles if we try that again," I explained.

Zara put her hands to her head. I knew she was anxious to find Synthia.

"Once we're on the highway, then how far until we get to planet Oliveria to pick up your ship?" I asked Stoller.

"We don't have to go there first. Let's go get your friend."

"Why the change?" asked Zara.

"Heck. I don't even know if Tristan still has that ship or if he sold it. Better to retrieve your friend as soon as possible. That's what you want, right?"

"Yeah, it is," said Zara.

"So, there you go," said Stoller. "It won't take long to travel to Mawzi. The Karakova Highway is fast. And I mean fast," he said as he lifted his newly attached arm and pointed his finger from one side of the window to another. "I'm starving. Anyone hungry?" He got up without waiting for any answers and headed off the bridge.

"Now that he mentioned it, I'm famished. Feti, I hope you can whip us up something tasty for dinner," Goggins said as he exited off the bridge.

"Why, yes, Dr. Goggins," Feti replied.

Zara slid out of the seat, "Come on, Gabe, join us."

I put the ship on auto-pilot with our course set to Lady Hypatia and left the bridge for the galley.

. . .

Dinner was jovial as everyone celebrated finding the Karakova Highway and Stoller's arm resurrection. There was a lively game of quinker after Stoller re-explained the rules of the game to us. And this gave him a chance to add a few more rules that helped him win more.

Honora, Talia and I were forbidden from using our telepathy skills during the game. Then Honora and I were caught counting cards, so Stoller said we had to reduce our mathematics directories to the skill level of a primary school-age Heragi. He said that leveled the playing field.

"Ahh!" yelled an excited Stoller as he won another round. He pulled in the lumpa chips that Feti made for us and had become the stand-in for our betting chips. It seemed that Edward Gates did not like games on his ship. Stoller said we were lucky that he always carried a deck of quinker cards with him everywhere he went.

It was good to see the Kell children laugh. And Zara and even Goggins were enjoying themselves.

Stoller got up and looked around the galley. He called out, "Feti, do you have any libations?"

"If you mean liquor or beer, Mr. Stoller, then yes. Mr. Gates has a large selection of any vintage from alien or humanoid distilleries. What would you like?" Feti replied.

"How about some Oliverian gin?" asked Stoller as he scratched his stubbly chin.

"Yes, it's illegal in the Heragi Empire, but Mr. Gates is very industrious and acquired a case on his last voyage," explained Feti.

"Excellent," said Stoller as he slapped his hands together and rubbed them. "Please retrieve me a bottle and some glasses, Feti."

Zara and Goggins sent Stoller a surprised look.

"What?" asked Stoller.

"Isn't that the providence of the prince who stole your ship?"

"Yeah, so what? He stole my ship, but his family makes an incredible gin that will blow your socks off."

The galley beverage door opened, and there was a green liquor bottle and six glasses on a tray. "Thank you, Feti," Stoller said with delight. He carried the tray over to the table.

The children's eyes widened.

Stoller poured out shots of the Oliverian gin into the glasses and passed them out.

"Um, the kids shouldn't drink," said Zara.

"There's no drinking age in the Edge. Age limits are only a Heragi rule. And we aren't in the Heragi Empire anymore," he replied with a grin.

"It's a good rule," said Zara as she whisked away the glasses from Honora and Talia who looked disappointed when she took them.

Alex grabbed his glass and gulped it down — and proceeded to cough. Everyone laughed, including Alex.

"Great, now your parents are going to hate me, too," said Zara, glancing at me.

My chest zinged with pain.

"Sorry, Gabe," said Zara. "I didn't mean to bring that up."

"That's okay," I said. It wasn't okay. But I didn't want Zara to feel bad. Like I felt. I hadn't thought of Ava since before the battle with Kaleb. But now she was back on my mind.

Talia leaned down from the end of the table and looked at me.

Everyone was silent.

Stoller looked around. "What? What am I missing? Why do your parents hate Gabe?"

"They don't both hate Gabe. Just their mother, Ava," said Goggins.

"Goggins, quiet," said Zara. She rolled her eyes, poured another shot of gin and drank it down.

"She'll get over it," said Talia's transceiver.

"It's my fault," said Honora. "Gabe was rescuing us from the Heragi military and was delivering us to our Uncle Jebediah on Zaradorba. We got Uncle Jeb on the *Alyssia* and then forced him and Gabe to take us to find our parents who were being held in prison."

"So, you all rescued your parents?" asked Stoller.

"Yes," answered Alex now that his coughing had subdued.

"I'd think they would be happy then," Stoller commented. "But the things that can trigger a female's fury — well, that subject I've been wrong on many, many times."

The children laughed along with Goggins and Zara. Stoller joined them with his large laughter.

I didn't laugh, but it made the pain in my chest subside a bit.

Once the laughter died down, Stoller looked at his empty glass and turned it upside down on the table. "I've heard of your Uncle Jeb, you know," he said to the children.

"You have?" asked Alex.

"Any enemies of the Heragi Empire are known at the Charbeaux Station," said Stoller. "We heard there was a skirmish on Zaradorba recently. I take it you were involved."

"You could say that," said Honora.

"Yeah, with your, um, special skills, I could see why the Heragi Empire wouldn't want you out of their sight," said Stoller. "Where's your uncle now?"

"We're not exactly sure. But I would assume he needs to get some of his rebel friends out of the Empire before Synthia —" Alex stopped talking and glanced at Zara. "Sorry."

"Before Synthia *what*? What is Synthia going to do?" asked Stoller.

"Synthia is a telepath. She also has the ability to know when someone is lying. Stefano drugged her, and that pulled down her resistance. She was able to read rebel captors' minds and reveal names of rebel moles in the Heragi government," explained Zara.

"My, that's awful," said Goggins, who glanced over to Talia.

Talia leaned into Honora, who put her arm around her.

"But Synthia won't out any more rebels," said Zara. "She was hanging on so she could meet the Kell children. To train them, which she did. She'll end her life before they force her to do that again. That's why I want to get to her as fast as we can."

"And they now have Gabe's code and our DNA samples," added Alex. "We need to destroy their lab."

"That's why we ran away. To help," said Honora. "Mom and Dad are worried, I'm sure. But Synthia trained us, as much as she could, in the short amount of time we had together."

Talia pushed her arm comm up into the air. "We are young but strong."

"The Heragi Empire wanted to imprison my parents and use us. We must stop them. Or they will never be stopped," said Honora.

"They'll continue to crush the freedom of all the people in their empire," added Zara.

Stoller pounded his glass on the table twice. "Here, here. I'm with you. All of you."

"What is our plan?" asked Goggins as he sipped his gin.

"We need to perform reconnaissance on the planet," I said. "Stoller, do you have any intel on the planet Mawzi?"

Stoller let out a deep breath. "It's a god-forsaken planet. A slight atmosphere. Red. Everything's red. Red dirt, red light. There is one metropolitan area — all under a dome."

"A dome?" asked Alex.

"Yeah, they need to manufacture atmosphere, air. They have an underground agriculture system. They make their rain in vast caves. I went there once. When I was in the military. We tried to rescue a soldier there, but it went sideways." He poured another shot.

"Who?" asked Goggins.

"One of the toughest, bravest fighters I ever knew," he said. "Her name was, or is, Anjori."

"A woman?" asked Honora.

"Yes, a woman. From the Oliveria Providence," he added.

"Oliveria?" said a surprised Goggins.

"That's where Tristan, your fellow quinker player, is from, isn't it?" asked Zara.

"Yes, that's his aunt. The ruler, Swina, that's Anjori's sister." He looked at his shot glass.

"My planet and Oliveria had an alliance years ago. Anjori was their military leader. A general. A great hero in countless battles. The Mawzi police had captured Anjori when her spaceship crashed on their planet. They saved her life but took her as a prisoner. Thought she was spying on them, which may or may not have been true. I don't know. All I know is that they had her."

Stoller took a deep breath.

"Me and a team were sent in, but they had her held deep in their caverns. I lost ten men before I called for a retreat. Me and two other crew members barely got back to our ship."

He drank another shot.

"Swina Oliveria never forgave me for abandoning her sister." Stoller looked over to me and nodded. "So, I know what it means to have a woman despise you."

"But you tried," said Honora.

"Sometimes trying isn't enough. Right, Gabe?" said Stoller.

Stoller kept digging into me like he knew me, like he somehow could relate to what I was going through. The man had had some experiences that hadn't been pleasant. His rough exterior and drinking didn't help when you immediately met him. But somehow a man that tries to connect with another, however awkward, must have some redemption inside him. And maybe I did too.

"Do you remember the caverns? That may be where they have Synthia. Where their lab could be located," said Zara.

"I have some recollection, but that was years ago. I'm sure they've dug deeper into their planet over the years."

Talia pushed her arm comm toward Stoller. "Do you think she's still alive?"

"Who? Anjori?" asked Stoller. Talia nodded. "I don't know. I don't know, kid. That was a long time ago."

Talia sent me a thought. *If Anjori is alive, we need to take her with us, too.*

I thought back to her, *If she is alive, we will, Talia.*

6

I was back on the bridge when Feti came over the comms. "Gabe, we're approaching Hypatia."

"Please contact Stoller, Feti. Ask him to come to the bridge."

"Copy that, Gabe."

Goggins sauntered in and sat down at his console. His hair was tousled and he yawned. "Morning, Gabe. I mean — what are you supposed to say in space?"

"Morning is fine, Dr. Goggins," I said.

The children filed in and took their seats. They all murmured hello in various ranges as they began to wake up.

Zara came in the most awake and excited. "Hello, everyone. Let's get this show on the road." She plopped into her seat and immediately pulled out her coder.

"Dr. Goggins, are you going to be mapping as we go?" I asked.

Goggins replied, "Yes, been doing that since we left Charbeaux Station. We may need it to get back."

"Good. We must be near the Karakova Highway," I said.

Everyone peered out of the bridge windows, but we couldn't see any sign of a highway.

"Zara, Goggins, Honora, are you picking up on any ship trails, reverb or energy residue?" I inquired.

They all reviewed their monitors.

"Nothing," said Goggins.

"Same," said Zara.

"Nope," said Honora.

"Keep trying," I said.

I heard Stoller's footsteps as he neared the bridge. He came in wiping his mouth from the meal he just finished. "Feti, whoa, you outdid yourself with breakfast this morning. I couldn't get enough of your spacecakes."

"Thank you, Stoller. That was Mr. Gates' children's favorite as well," said Feti.

Stoller took the co-commander's seat. He scratched his chin as he looked at Hypatia. Then he put his fingers up in the air. He changed his finger directions in various ways and configurations. He hemmed and hawed.

"Are you using your fingers to navigate?" asked Goggins.

"Yes, in a manner," Stoller replied.

"We're being guided by finger puppets?" asked Zara.

Stoller spun around to face her. "Dr. Goggins, look on your navigation screen. Type in coordinates forty-five lats and sixty-four-zero-nine. Got it?"

"Got it," said Goggins as he typed the coordinates into the system. He waited. "They're in."

Stoller turned to me. "Okay, follow those coordinates, and we'll enter the highway."

I began to steer toward the coordinates that Goggins entered into the system.

"This is an invisible highway?" asked Zara.

"Yes. Sort of. I didn't believe it the first time either," said Stoller. "Gabe, one more thing. Do you have infrared lights?"

"Yes," I said.

"Put them on," he said and leaned back in his chair.

I punched in the commands and turned on the infrared lights on the exterior of the *Alyssia*.

The lights illuminated what looked like a current. Small spaceships and large freighters passed in front of us. The kids all let out an excited shout.

"I see ships!" exclaimed Goggins.

Stoller laughed.

"Amazing," said Alex.

"You travel at two-g speed once you drop in," he said.

"How come we couldn't see those ships before?" asked Honora.

"The highway has essentially a natural stealth harmonic frequency causing it to be cloaked to the bare eye," explained Stoller.

"Cool," replied Honora.

Talia pushed her way to the front of the window. She was smiling, and I could sense her wonderment as she looked out at the highway.

Stoller spun around. "What do you think, Zara?"

"I like that it's fast."

Stoller smiled. "Oh, it's fast. Hang on to your hats. Okay, Gabe, ease the *Alyssia* in," he directed me.

"Everyone take your seats and buckle up," I said.

I pushed the ship forward, and we entered the Karakova Highway with a bump. Then we were pulled into the flow of the entrance lane. We were thrown forward and then back into our seats.

Stoller let out a yip of enjoyment.

"I can't control our speed," I said as the ship accelerated.

"No, you can't. The highway is in charge of the speed," he said.

"How do we know the ship can handle it?" asked Zara.

"I never saw a ship break up on the highway. It just knows," said Stoller.

"*It* knows?" said Goggins. "That sounded like *it's* alive."

"It is," said Stoller flatly.

"That's hard to believe," said Goggins under his breath.

Stoller leaned over to Goggins. "We got a robot that can feel and a kid who can tell if a person is lying, a girl who can heal a severed arm and a kid who can throw objects around like they're nothing with his mind. Now tell me, is a highway that is of a higher intelligence really that hard to believe?"

"Now that you put it like that, I guess not," said Goggins.

Stoller laughed. "I don't mean to be harsh on you, Doc, but the Edge is a wondrous and mind-blowing area. I'm still seeing new things all the time." He twirled around and smiled as he looked out onto the highway.

The g-force suddenly eased, and we could move around normally.

"What? Are we slowing down?" asked Goggins.

"It's easier to move," said Alex as he pulled up from his seat.

"Aren't we doing 2-g?" asked Zara.

"We are. But all ships and their inhabitants adjust automatically. It's called the Zambler Effect. Nice, huh?"

I looked down at my console. Indeed, my instruments reported that we're traveling at 2-g. Amazing.

"Who is Zambler?" I asked.

"Some crazy Edger pioneer. He brought his family out here centuries ago. He found the highway and then from generation to generation, it's been passed down to Edgers how to find the highway and how it works. Nothing's written down about it. Isn't that great?"

"As a scientist, no, I think that's abhorrent," said Goggins.

I monitored Stoller's bio-metrics. They were rising. Not due to fear but excitement. He truly enjoyed being in the Edge and traveling on the Karakorva Highway.

It warmed my chest. I was glad he could enjoy himself. We didn't know what we would meet on Mawzi, and any sense of happiness in space should be savored. I wished I could feel that warmth longer, but it began to go away as soon as I felt it.

We'd traveled for over two hours on the highway when Goggins spoke. "Stoller's coordinates to Mawzi are triggering. We're getting close."

"We sure are," said Stoller. "Gabe, see that planet off our starboard?" He pointed.

"The red one?"

"That's it. That's Mawzi," he said as he straightened up in his chair. "Take the next exit."

I steered the ship off the exit as Stoller directed me, and we pushed forward in our seats as our speed immediately declined. The kids jolted awake.

"Oomph. A little warning next time, Gabe," said Honora as she rubbed her head.

"Sorry," I said. "We have Mawzi off our starboard."

Everyone got up to take a closer look at the red planet with swirling colors around it.

"What are the swirls?" asked Honora.

"Winds. High winds," said Stoller.

We were getting closer, and Stoller directed our coordinates to the main populace location on the planet.

"You'll need to bring the *Alyssia* in fast and travel low until we get near the dome," Stoller advised.

"Back in your seats," I ordered.

We lowered easily down to the surface with the thin atmosphere, but the winds jostled us about. We were hit hard by a gust. I struggled to keep us straight. Everyone lurched left and right.

"Lower. Get lower," said Stoller.

I descended the *Alyssia* even farther. The winds died down. I cruised us around red mountains and expanses. We came upon enormous sand dunes.

A large dome could be seen in the distance. It had hundreds of medium and small sized domes huddled around it.

"Impressive," said Zara as she stared at the domed city in the distance.

"How did they build it?" asked Alex.

"From the inside out. The Mawzi weren't always underground dwellers. They once had a normalized atmosphere. But they got caught in the cross fires of a nuclear war that caused havoc. They had to survive in their caves for thousands of years before they were able to build the domes."

"Who sent in the nukes?" asked Goggins.

"The Oliverians. Anjori and Swina's ancestors. It was an accident. I mean, not the war but the missiles got misdirected here. That is why the Mawzians hate the Oliverians."

"I don't blame them," said Honora.

Stoller nodded. "Yeah, but do you really have to pay for the sins of your father or your mother?" asked Stoller as he looked back toward Honora.

"Copy that," said Honora as she sat back in her seat, undoubtedly thinking of her parents.

Stoller pointed. "Over there. Put her down over there," he said. We set down behind a large red rocky hill, hoping we weren't detected.

"How do we get in?" asked Zara.

"There was a vent opening on this hill when I was last here. I hope it's still there," said Stoller. "Feti, did you say Mr. Gates had children?"

"Yes, seven," replied Feti.

"Good. That means there's children sized spacesuits in the cargo bay, correct?" asked Stoller.

"That is correct," replied Feti.

"Seven? Whoa, he has a large brood. I mean family," Stoller said as he smiled at the children.

"We won't need them," I said.

"What?" said Stoller.

"The Kell children aren't getting off this ship," I said.

All of the children cried out in protest.

"Gabe, that's why we came," said Honora as she spun around in her chair.

"I'm almost eighteen, so technically I'm almost an adult. And I helped rescue Mom and Dad on our last trip," Alex retorted.

Talia threw her arm comm up in the air for us to hear. "Gabe, thank you for your concern, but we want to help. We demand to help."

I weighed their protests and thought of Ava and Damiel, who would not want them to be in harm's way. I must protect them. That was my prime directive.

"If they want to help, then let them help," said Zara.

I weighed Zara's reasoning, but her closeness to Synthia may be clouding her judgement.

I felt Talia in my head. *Let Alex go with you. And Honora. I will stay back at the ship.*

I sent a thought back to her. *But I'm compromising my prime directive. And your mother will hate me more than she does now. Rightly so.*

Maybe. But you have to stop thinking of her.

I'll try.

We've outgrown your prime directive.

I don't want that to be true.

We're not normal children.

No, you're not normal, are you?

And we never will be.

"Well?" Stoller inquired louder. I pulled myself out of the telepathic conversation that Talia and I were having.

"Alex will go down to Mawzi," I said.

"Not fair," started Honora who jumped up in protest.

I held up my hand. "And Honora, too." She sat down and smiled at Alex, who gave her a thumbs up. "Talia will stay here with Dr. Goggins,"

"Very good, Gabe. That make sense," said Goggins. He ran his fingers through his hair and let out a breath of relief.

"Stoller, Zara and I will be on point. Then Honora and Alex will be sweep," I concluded.

"Copy that," said Alex with a grin. He was looking forward to the possible battle. I would need to keep a watch on that. I didn't want him to like fighting too much. There's a difference between wanting to rescue someone close to you and wanting to kill for the sake of killing.

"Let's suit up," I ordered. Everyone but Talia and Goggins left for the back of the ship.

In the suit chamber, Stoller helped Alex put on an atmospheric suit, and Zara helped Honora. Alex had had training in atmospheric suits at the military academy, but putting on one of these suits was all new for Honora. So was walking in a thin atmosphere and lighter gravity.

We had stocked up with weapons and each picked their favorite gun. Honora chose the same gun style that I preferred. That must be due to the military combat code we now shared. She nodded and gave me a small smile when I watched her attach the gun to her suit holster.

"Good taste," I said.

Stoller grabbed two backpacks and stuffed a suit in each one. He handed me one of the packs and donned one for himself.

"Suits for Anjori and Synthia," he said. "Hopefully, we will need them."

When everyone was done, I checked their suits' air levels, temp system and comms. All were working appropriately. I, of course, didn't need a suit but had to adjust down my sensors for heat and pain due to the heat and radiation exposure in the thin atmosphere.

"Everyone in the airlock," I said.

I could see a bit of hesitation in Honora's eyes.

"Everyone, okay?" I asked, putting my fist and thumb up in the air. They held up their thumbs for the okay sign.

"Open the hatch, Feti," I ordered.

"Affirmative, Gabe. Good luck."

"Visors down," I ordered. "Thanks, Feti. Stoller, lead the way."

We marched down the ramp, and everyone pulled down their dark visors as they adjusted to the blaring red sun. We pushed against the wind and sand swirling around us.

"This way," said Stoller as he waved us to the side of the red hill. We scrambled over the rocks and came upon a large circular lid six feet wide in diameter. "This is it," yelled Stoller over the wind. "Vacuum sealed."

I crouched and felt the lid, trying to find a place to grip it. I came across an edge with a ridge. I pulled slightly to see how heavy it was. It was heavy. I leaned down and steadied myself and put my fingers underneath and began lifting with all my strength. I'd gotten it up a foot when I started to falter a bit. It was too heavy for me. Then I felt support.

It was Honora, lifting to the right of me. She was tapping into her strength code.

"I got it," I said as I felt the vacuum from below try to hold the lid closed. We were able to lift it three feet up.

Stoller yelled, "Everyone in, quick. Hold it open, Gabe."

Everyone who slid near the entrance of the tunnel got sucked in. I was the last one in. I crawled under the lid and started getting pulled downward. The lid was falling.

I heard a *bang* — it caught my right arm. I was caught dangling. The pain was excruciating, even with my pain sensors pulled down to their minimum.

"Ahh," I yelled.

The team was strewn upon the floor ten feet below. I couldn't get enough leverage to push the lid up with my one free arm.

Honora jumped to her feet. "Alex, throw me up toward Gabe."

Alex concentrated on Honora, then raised both his arms and flew her up toward me. I caught her with my left arm. "Oooph," she grunted as she hit my chest.

She climbed up on my shoulder and pushed on the lid. It began to move.

"One more push," she yelled as she exerted all her strength.

The lid moved, freed my arm and we both fell to the floor.

"Ow," Honora grunted. She got up and rubbed her backside. "You okay, Gabe?"

I checked out my arm and slowly got up. I had some exterior damage, but my arm was functional.

"I'm okay. Thanks, Honora," I said.

"Sure," she said as she checked her weapon.

Stoller led us into an airlock chamber. And after a few moments, they were able to take off their helmets and breathe freely. They took off their suits, and we left the backpacks near the chamber.

We proceeded to a nearby tunnel. It was lit with minimal security lights that gave off a green hue. The Mawzis probably appreciated different colored lights than the eternal red rolling mountains and dunes.

The cavernous air smelled like dirt but with a smoky spice. It didn't smell bad. In fact, according to my odor sensors, it registered as pleasant. I don't know how else to describe it beyond that it smelled real. Organic. More so than I ever experienced on Heragi or of course the Charbeaux Station.

"Hopefully, that lid opening will only be a blip on a Mawzi security screen. Let's get moving. This way," said Stoller as he started running down the tunnel.

We all followed Stoller as the tunnel descended deeper into the red caverns of Mawzi.

7

As we descended into the tunnels of Mawzi, we were able to see the vast industrious nature of their civilization that went back thousands of years. We came upon huge cathedral-like buildings in vast ravines that were multiple stories.

"Magnificent," said Zara as she marveled at the carved stone behemoth structures. There were hieroglyphs engraved in the walls. We got near enough to admire their ancient stories that captured the Mawzian religious and societal stories and rituals.

"The Mawzians are expert builders and architects. They have to be, to live thousands of years in the ground," said Stoller as he looked up to a particularly breathtaking structure.

"Is this a church?" asked Alex.

"Looks like it. The Mawzians worship many different gods. But I do know the biggest thing they worship is work. Tunnel-making takes a lot of resources," said Stoller. "And these took centuries."

Alex and Zara wondered at the ceiling and the carvings.

"Do they mine precious metals?" asked Zara.

"No, nothing to mine on Mawzi except dirt. That's what they

sell across the galaxy to substations wanting to form agriculture stations. Terraforming is big business."

"Isn't that a finite supply?" I asked.

"Yes, but they don't care. Even if it could de-stabilize their planet's core. Their biggest problem is that people are in finite supply. There were rumors of slave labor. Of course, the Mawzian leaders have always denied it," said Stoller as he surveyed his comm unit for a directional signal.

I watched Honora walk up to the church-like building and touch it. She closed her eyes. I didn't want to intrude into her mind, but actually I did want to intrude. I concentrated and went inside.

She was reaching out and talking with a small Mawzi girl. The girl was pale and small. Her eyes were sunken into her skull. Honora turned to me in her mind. *She wants our help.*

"Gabe! Gabe!" yelled Stoller. "Time to go."

I snapped out of Honora's mind. She pulled her hands away from the structure.

"Right behind you," I said as I waved to everyone to follow.

We hiked down for miles. The temperature rose as we neared the bottom of the city center. The tunnels became more sophisticated, from dirt walls to fortified walls with metal beams. We didn't detect any security.

"What about cameras or tripping security sensors?" asked Alex.

Stoller stopped. "Not in this area. I mean, they had all that, but it was turned off ten years ago. At least it was when I was here."

"Why?" asked Zara.

"They stopped utilizing this section," Stoller said.

"Yeah, but why?" asked Zara.

"There was a contamination," he said. "A gas from the core

leaked into this area. Killed a lot of Mawzians. They had to seal it off."

"You led us into a contaminated area?" said Zara with irritation. "Thanks for the heads-up."

"Gabe?" asked Alex.

I scanned and reviewed the air properties. "The air quality is fine. My system shows no contamination or at least no harmful trace gasses."

"See?" said Stoller. "It's had ten years to dissipate."

"Thanks for your concern," said Zara.

"Are we going to keep jabbing, or are we going to rescue your friend?" asked Stoller.

"And your friend, too," added Honora.

"Yeah, if she's alive," he said as he turned to resume walking forward.

We continued downward and began to hear the humming of machinery.

"Air production. Probably some power production too," said Stoller as we all stopped to listen. "This way. We're close. There should be a utility ladder coming up."

We moved forward a few more yards and turned a corner. There it was — a ladder leading upward.

"Is this how you made your way in and out when you were last here?" asked Alex.

"Just the way in. We escaped through their planet-port station," said Stoller.

"How did you get back to your navy ship?" asked Alex.

"We didn't. We had to leave it here," Stoller explained.

"You stole one of their ships?" said Zara.

"We didn't have much of a choice," said Stoller.

"How many ships have you stolen in your lifetime?" asked Alex.

"Kid, you ask a lot of questions, you know that? *A few.* Any more questions before we go and try to save your friend and take on the whole Mawzi establishment?" Stoller asked.

"No, I'm good." Alex backed up a few steps.

"Okay, then," said Stoller as he began climbing the ladder.

I changed up our positions and had Alex follow Stoller and then Zara and Honora with me taking the sweep position. If anyone was going to surprise us from behind, I could provide more coverage with my armor. That was the least I could do to protect the Kell children as more guilt started to kick in while we ascended the ladder.

We climbed up to the next level, and Stoller found a floor panel that we were able to access. We surfaced on the forty-fourth floor of the Mawzi substation system.

Alex peered at a wall panel. It had bumps on it. He touched them.

Zara followed behind him and reached out and touched the bumps on the wall panel as well. "It's a language. It's a braille system."

"Are the Mawzians blind?" asked Honora.

Stoller nodded. "Some of them are. Many of the working class. They've been working for generations down in the caves and low light. That's one of the reasons they wanted to build their dome system."

"So their people wouldn't go blind?" asked Honora.

"So their *rich* people don't go blind," he said. "They have a rotation system. Every rich family that can afford it pays for a year living under the dome. Their bodies soak up the sunlight and then back down into their basement apartments they go."

"But the workers?" Honora asked.

Stoller shook his head. "No. They hardly get to go up to the dome. If they do, it's because of a delivery or because they're servants."

Honora threw me a thought. *The girl.*

I sent her a thought back. *We need to stay focused.*

Honora nodded. I felt a pain in my chest. There was a sadness in her eyes, and I reviewed her bio-levels. They were dipping. That may be expected on a mission like this, but I felt a confliction in her growing. I would have to watch her more carefully than I thought.

I wasn't sure what the image of the little Mawzi girl in Honora's mind was exactly. It could have been Honora's mind playing tricks or old energy from the caves. Only Synthia could tell us for sure.

Now that Honora had telepathic gifts entangled with my code, and all the attributes I had, she may overestimate her ability and take risks that she couldn't overcome. She still, after all, is an adolescent.

With strength and knowledge can come over-confidence. That may be okay for a robot, but her body parts were human, and she could still be severely injured. None of us knew if she could self-heal.

We weren't here to unravel the Mawzians' whole society. We couldn't save everyone from whatever caste system they had established for generations here. And if Stoller couldn't rescue an Oliverian war hero from these cave depths with a full navy platoon, then our mission was even more precarious.

An elevator was at the end of the hallway.

"Zara, we need your coding skills here," said Stoller as he hit the dead elevator buttons.

Zara pulled out her coder and began to hack into its utility program. She smiled and showed her coder screen as it turned green. The door opened.

"What took you so long?" said Stoller as he entered the elevator. Zara slammed her coder into her utility belt.

Alex chuckled and then Zara shot him a look. "Sorry, Zara. He's teasing you."

"Yeah, I know. Grade school techniques do not amuse me." She strode into the elevator.

"Noted," said Stoller as he punched the button to take us up a level.

"What's next?" I asked.

"We have to go up and get some intel on where they could be holding Synthia," said Stoller. "These tunnels go on for hundreds of miles. We need information."

"And what about Anjori?" asked Honora.

"She was being held in a building under the dome when I was here. I'm sure after our failed attempt, they moved her down deep."

The elevator door opened. Stoller drew his weapon and peeked out of the elevator. "Clear," he announced. We moved out. He searched for a utility room. "We're right below the commerce station. We'll be able to blend in with the dirt traders and flight operators."

"I'm a robot. How do I blend?" I asked.

He laughed. "Yes, you are a robot. Don't worry, plenty of bots are here with the trading companies to help with cargo and logistics — and for guarding the rich traders. Just look tough."

Tough?

Alex laughed. Oh, he was joking. Alex was becoming a fan of Stoller's. I hoped he didn't pick up on his sense of humor. It was only tolerable from Stoller.

"What about our guns?" asked Zara as she held hers up.

"They open carry on Mawzi. Just don't make a hole in the dome if we get into a firefight. You don't want to be responsible for killing four million Mawzians and visitors, do you?"

"Um, no," she said.

"Just kidding. The dome material can't be harmed by bullets or laser guns. At least from the inside." He got back in the elevator. We all piled in. "Next stop, the Mawzian open market." He hit the button and the door closed.

· · ·

In a few seconds, we were on the ground level under the dome. The elevator door opened up to a packed crowd of Mawzians, aliens, bots and humanoids hustling to and from the various levels under the main dome and linked domes.

We exited and looked around in wonderment. The dome was hundreds of stories high. Giant shades moved with the direction of the Mawzian solar sun. Huge swaths of colored banners of gold and green and flapping shades helped cool the inside of the dome. It was actually quite pleasant inside.

Mawzian barter men yelled in different alien languages as multiple auctions were taking place for dirt of various grades. The audience hovered around the auctioneers who held up their hand monitors with holograms that showed rising bids as traders typed in offers that alerted the auctioneers.

Shops and booths lined the streets, selling agriculture supplies, seeds and plants of all varieties.

Wealthy Mawzian families strolled by with an air of dignity as they seated themselves in nearby cafes and took rikshaws to travel from dome to dome powered by working class Mawzians.

"Where to now?" I asked.

"Where do you go for any information?" said Stoller.

"Let me guess. A bar," said Zara as she gave Stoller a hard glance.

"Correct. You pick up on things quickly, don't you?" joked Stoller as he continued down the street. He stopped and questioned an alien, who was happy to oblige. Stoller turned back to us. "This way to the nearest pilot libation center."

"Um, what about Honora and Alex?" asked Zara.

"What? There's no drinking age on Mawzi. I told you that already. They're fine," he said as he strode down the street.

Zara pointed her finger at Alex. "No Oliverian gin for you."

Alex smiled. "I don't work and drink."

She gave him a look.

"Just kidding," Alex said as he raised his hands in innocence.

Honora pulled me back from the group. "Look over there."

I followed her gaze and saw a group of traders walk into another dome that was blackened out. There were beleaguered Mawzians wearing chains. They were hustled through a separate door that also led into the dome.

I sighed. She heard it.

"It's a slave auction, isn't it?" she asked.

"Yes," I said. "Come, we need to follow Stoller."

Honora moved away from my grip and headed toward the darkened dome. She weaved in and out of the crowd.

"Honora!" I yelled and then realized I shouldn't be making a commotion. I ported into her mind.

Come back here!

Tell Stoller I'll catch up with him.

I'm not leaving you alone out here.

Afraid of what Mother will do?

I could sense her laugh a bit.

Always, I thought as I followed her and sent a message to Stoller that we would catch up with him.

Honora approached the Mawzian guard granting access into the darkened dome. She flashed a galaxy card and nodded to me. The guard let us both in.

We headed down into a vestibule that led to the darkened dome. Potential customers pushed past us.

Where did you get your own galaxy card? I asked.

Zara showed me how to hack into the Suissey bank. I created a new identity. Don't you know I'm a millionaire? On digital script at least. She smiled as she waved the card and then put it in her pocket.

Our eyes adjusted to the low yellow lights that lit the stage where there was an auctioneer's podium. It was arena seating. We found two seats in the back. There were at least fifteen different alien languages that my syntax picked up on. I looked around the dome to assess the guard situation. There wasn't much security presence. Two guards at the entrance and two stationed at the stage door.

Honora hit my chest with her elbow. I wished she wouldn't do that. She nodded toward the door on the stage as it opened.

A group of twenty Mawzians was ushered on the stage. Adult males and one female and one child. They were all very pale, and their eyes were sunken. They were blind. They were diggers.

The auctioneer approached his pulpit and began the bidding process. There was a hologram auction board on the wall that lit up with numbers circulating upward as audience members bid on the first male.

The Mawzian up for sale looked at the floor. He was wiry and dirty. My chest began to hurt as we witnessed the barbaric slave auction.

"Come, come," said the auctioneer. "This digger is one of our finest specimens. He will give you a return on your investment in your mining operations so quick it will make your head spin. Or in the case of our Galugian alien friends, your multiple heads spin."

Honora sent me a thought. *There's the girl.*

I scanned the Mawzians up for sale. Standing off to the side was a young girl holding what I presumed was her mother's hand. Her mother looked tired but held her daughter's hand firmly.

The male was sold. The auctioneer rang his bell and called up the next Mawzian. The guards ushered up another male, but the auctioneer shook his head and pointed to the girl and her mother.

"I have a mother-daughter team of diggers. They can work in your caves and help with any inside servant duties. Truly a two-for-one deal. Let us begin," he said with delight.

The guards pulled the woman and her daughter across the stage. The mother lost her balance and fell. She stayed on her knees and hugged her daughter. They were frightened. I wanted to run up to the stage and wipe out the whole crowd with my gun. I refrained.

Honora put her arm across my chest. She had read my thought.

Numbers flew upward on the auction board. They were a popular item to bid on, apparently.

Honora pulled out her coder and her galaxy card. She began pounding. She was bidding on the mother-daughter.

Every time the bid went higher, she matched it.

The auctioneer was delighted. He tried to peer out into the crowd to see who the final bidders were. Honora slammed in the final bid. The auctioneer granted them to her.

"Congratulations." He looked down on his pad. "Won by Nora, is that correct?"

The auctioneer raised his hands for the dome lights to brighten over the crowd. We were now illuminated. People clapped. Honora stood and waved. She was playing the part of Nora. The mother-daughter were ushered into the back room behind the stage.

Follow me, thought Honora.

We rose and headed to the stage door. The guard let us in when they saw it was Honora who had just purchased the mother-daughter.

In the back, there were more Mawzians ready for auction. I took an assessment again of the security guards. There were two in this small holding room.

What is your plan? I thought. *We need to find Synthia. Any commotion here could jeopardize that.*

I don't know. I just couldn't let anyone else buy and take her and her mother.

We don't even have enough spacesuits to get them to our ship.

I know. I know. Let me think.

A guard led us to the mother-daughter. He handed Honora a

light chain that secured their hands together. Honora could hardly take the chain. The guard walked away.

The mother lowered her head. "We are hard workers. We won't cause any trouble. But we won't be separated. Please."

"Follow me," said Honora as she led them out of the room into the open market, where she stopped and turned to them. "I won't separate you. And I won't be your owner either. I'm going to get you off this planet."

I made a perimeter scan to make sure we weren't drawing attention to us.

The mother was confused. The daughter looked up and smiled. "I know you. I saw you." Honora kneeled, and the little girl touched her face. "You told me not to be afraid."

"Yes, that was me," said Honora.

"Are you going to re-sell us?" asked the mother.

"No. I'm going to release you," said Honora.

"Where?" asked the mother.

"I don't know. I don't even know how I'll get you off the planet," said Honora.

"Return us. We don't want any trouble," said the mother in fear.

"Mom, no," said the girl.

"What are your names?" asked Honora.

"I'm Meeor, and this is my daughter Belin," the mother said.

"Meeor, I'm not trying to get you in trouble. I'm trying to save you from being slaves," said Honora.

"Why?" asked the mother.

"Some people wanted to enslave me and my sister and brother. I hate anyone who wants to enslave another," Honora explained.

"There are many Mawzian slaves," said the mother. "We are but two."

"I know," said Honora. She took a deep breath. Honora knew

she couldn't save them all. At least not right now. "One day, I'll come back."

"How did you escape?" asked the girl.

"This robot with me. He stole a ship," Honora said as she looked off and then back to the girl. I read Honora's thought. She was looking for signs to the planet-port. She was going to steal a ship. Oh, boy.

"Gabe, go back to Stoller. I'll meet up with you," said Honora as she took the chains off the mother and daughter.

"Where are you going?"

"You know where I'm going. You read my thought."

"The planet-port."

Honora smiled. "I'm a pretty good pilot, you know."

"I know. You're as good as me."

She touched my arm and then took the mother and daughter by the hands and led them away.

I watched them weave through the crowd until they were out of sight. My chest hurt. Ouch. I rubbed it and then pulled down my arm before anyone could notice my reflex.

The Kell children would be the death of me.

I turned to go back and find Stoller and the rest of our team.

8

────────

I activated my arm comm to contact Stoller to find their location. He directed me to a bar off a side street on the second floor. I felt a bit self-conscious walking by myself through the Mawzian streets. There were other bots in the crowd, but they were either guard-bots or service-bots that had travel directives from their owners, as far as I could tell. They were retrieving either children from school or goods from stores.

One guard-bot looked at me and gave me a ping. It was an Ameribot Industries robot. I pinged back my non-descript reply which contained a directive from a fictional Mawzian owner with orders to pick up garments from a dress shop. We exchanged nods as we passed each other.

If its owner knew that their guard-bot was more self-actualized than reported by Ameribot, where Ava and Damiel had worked and created me, then they would be shocked out of their garments. I didn't know if I wanted to explain that fully to the Kells. It would probably scare the heck out of them. I tabled those thoughts as I turned down an alley to the bar.

It was called Swift Zuri. I looked up the word Zuri on the Mawzian outernet. Apparently, it was a mythological bird that used to fly in the red skies of Mawzi. A large blue and green bird adorned the door, which seemed pretty fitting for a pilot bar. I opened the door and entered the smoke-filled room. This wasn't a healthy environment for Alex, but it was too late now. I adjusted my eyesight levels and entered.

Stoller, Zara and Alex sat at a table that had beverages already on it. I didn't like that I saw a drink in front of Alex. I hoped it wasn't alcoholic. In fact, I hoped all the drinks weren't alcoholic considering we needed to be sharp, but I knew that was a low possibility for Stoller's drink.

I took a seat.

"Where's Honora?" asked a concerned Alex.

How could I explain this without sounding like a complete guardian failure?

"She's headed to the planet-port. She's safe," I said.

"Why is she going there?" asked Zara.

"She rescued two Mawzians sold into slavery. She plans on stealing a spaceship," I said in a low voice.

"What? How did she rescue them?" asked Zara.

"She bought them," I said.

Zara slammed her drink down. "I appreciate Honora's heart-felt action, but this jeopardizes us rescuing Synthia."

"Unless I was going to pick her up and drag her over here, she was determined," I explained.

"Gabe is right there," said Alex.

"Way to watch over her. I can see why Ava is angry at you, letting her kids do anything they want while endangering themselves and others," snapped Zara.

Ouch, that comment sent a pain to my chest.

"Zara, I know Honora better than anyone. Once she gets something in her head, there is no stopping her," defended Alex.

Stoller shook his head and took a swig of his drink. "Enough. She's seems to be a pretty capable young lady, but her timing stinks." He looked around the room and spotted two Mawzian army pilots. They were in green uniforms with the Mawzian flag and their military rankings on their sleeves.

Stoller signaled for the waitress, and a Mawzian woman approached us. "Me and my friends will pay for the drinks of those two military fly-boys over there, okay, miss?"

She nodded. "You're very generous. Are you staying on Mawzi long, handsome?"

Stoller smiled. "I may. I find everyone here so friendly — and beautiful," he said as he raised his drink to her. The waitress winked and then shot a look at Zara before leaving.

Zara put her fingers in her drink and flicked the contents at Stoller. "Really? You have to flirt with the waitress now?"

"It helps to be friendly to everyone when you're trying to get some intel," he explained as he wiped Zara's drink off his face. "And what? Are you jealous?"

Zara was about to respond to Stoller when Alex leaned in. "Hey, guys. Can you stop your bickering for like five minutes?"

Zara leaned back.

We watched the waitress bring the pilots two new drinks. She pointed toward our table and the pilots hoisted their drinks up as an acknowledgement. Stoller did the same.

"And when does the information flow begin?" asked Zara.

Stoller ate one of the snacks from the bowl on the table. "Patience, patience."

In a few minutes, the pilots left their bar stools.

"They're coming toward us," reported Alex.

The pilots headed straight for our table with their refreshments in hand.

Stoller smiled and lifted his drink toward Zara. "See?" He looked up and smiled as the two pilots leaned over our table.

"Thank you for the drinks," said the taller pilot. "Appreciate it."

"We appreciate you keeping Mawzi safe," said Stoller as he toasted the pilot.

The pilot eyed everyone at the table. He smiled at Zara who struggled to smile back. He motioned for his shorter co-pilot to grab a chair which he did and sat next to me.

"Where are you from?" asked the tall pilot.

"Clete. Shopping for some dirt," said Stoller.

"And slaves," I added.

Stoller's eyes widened. My additional conversation builder was not appreciated.

"Name's Jablo. This is Nei," said the tall pilot.

"Nice to meet you," said Stoller.

"Dirt and slaves, huh?" said Jablo. "Best dirt and slaves in the Edge."

"That's what we hear. It's our first time here," said Zara.

"Welcome," said Jablo as he raised his glass.

"Let us know if you need any restaurant or entertainment suggestions," said Nei. "The planet aims to keep their guests comfortable."

The pilots laughed. I didn't like their laugh. Even my grunt-like laugh was better than theirs any day of the week.

Stoller faked a smile. "Come to think of it, we bought some slaves and asked them to hold them for us. But we're a little turned around in all these domes. Where exactly can we pick them up?"

"All the holding cells are in the fourth-floor sub-level under the teleport," said Jablo.

"Really?" said Stoller.

"Yeah, for easy planet-port transport," said Jablo.

"And where would I find a medical bay?" asked Zara. The pilots looked at her.

"Is there something wrong?" asked Nei.

"My son—" she said, pointing to Alex.

"If he is sick, he needs to be quarantined. That's the rule here," said Nei as he stared at Alex.

"He cut his knee earlier. I just want to make sure it's okay," said Zara as she put her hand on Alex who started rubbing his left knee.

"Our medbay is in city-center in the main-dome. They will be able to take a look at it," said Jablo.

"You guys see much action these days?" asked Stoller.

"Nah, pretty quiet lately," said Jablo.

"Still warring with the Oliveria Providence?"

"Nei and I had a little skirmish with one of their cruisers a few weeks ago. But things have been quiet," said Jablo.

"I'd love for something to get started. The Oliverians are the curse of this galaxy," said Nei. "If they think they're busting into the dome, they're crazy."

"When did they do that? I mean, this dome does look pretty secure," said Zara.

"It is. A few years ago, they tried," said Jablo.

"It was a massive failure," said Nei.

I gathered the pilots were talking about Stoller's attempt to rescue Anjori.

Stoller twisted in his chair. "They must have had a good reason. To try such a foolish thing."

"Yeah, we got something they want," said Nei as he drank more.

"What? Tech?" asked Alex.

"No, kid," said Jablo as he finished his drink. "We got one of their generals."

Stoller waved his hand to signal the waitress to bring the pilots another round on him.

Nei laughed. "Crazy. I heard she's eight feet tall."

"I heard they cut off her legs so now she's just four feet tall," said Jablo with a laugh.

Okay, I didn't like these pilots at all. Zara frowned and then recovered her facial appearance. Stoller's face didn't flinch. In fact, he laughed with them. Boy, he was good. He must be seething inside.

"Geez, I would love to see that. Put her on display, eh?" said Stoller. The pilots grunted and agreed.

"Yeah, that would teach those Oliverians a lesson," said Nei.

"I bet you got her locked up pretty secure, right? I hope so," said Stoller.

"She's deep down in our caverns," said Nei.

"No, I heard she got moved," said Jablo.

"Yeah?" asked Nei.

The waitress delivered the pilots more drinks. They each took long swigs.

"Yep, it's true. Doing some freaky experiments on her," said Jablo as he gulped down his drink.

Nei slapped Alex on the back. "When you're at the medbay, you may be able to sneak a peek." Nei and Jablo laughed.

"That would be great," said Alex, playing along.

"I mean, that is, if you can get by our special ops team. Fat chance of that," said Nei.

"Yeah, those are some bad blasters," said Jablo.

"I guess we'll just stick to the first floor," said Zara with a smile.

"Yeah, the fifth sub-floor is no place for a lady or a kid," said Jablo.

"You got that right. I heard of some pretty wicked things they do to slave freers down there," said Nei.

"Slave freers?" I asked.

"Yeah," said Jablo. "A lot of off-planet folks come here pretending to buy slaves but they're buying them to set them free. Bunch of idiots. They take the freers down there for interrogation."

"There's a whole underground network of the freers," added Nei. "Probably in cahoots with the Heragi Empire."

"Heragi?" asked Zara.

"Yeah, those Heragi are so full of themselves. They've been

meeting with our planet officials. Who knows what's brewing with them," said Jablo.

"How do you catch the freers?" asked Stoller.

Jablo laughed and pulled out his gun and pointed it at his face. "You're not one of them, are you?"

We all froze.

Stoller laughed. "Heck no. I just drained my galaxy account for five prime slaves. I need to get my return-on-investment." Stoller pushed Jablo's gun to the side playfully.

Jablo and Nei laughed and slapped each other in the gut.

"Yeah, you don't look like freers. They're morons with whiny speeches about freedom and everyone being equal," said Nei.

I did a quick bio-scan of Zara since her jawline tightened. Her adrenaline was rising along with her impulse levels.

Time to go.

Stoller finished up his drink and pushed away from the table. "Boys, nice to chat with you. Thanks again for making the skies safe for us. I feel so much better after talking with you both."

Stoller, Zara, Alex and I rose to leave.

"Yeah, thanks for the drinks, mate," said Jablo.

"Take care of your arm, kid," said Nei.

Alex grabbed his right arm and grinned. "Yeah, will do."

We left the table and headed into the street.

"It was your left knee not your arm," I reminded Alex.

Alex whipped around to face me. "Do you think they noticed?"

"Nah, they were pretty snockered, kid," said Stoller as he rambled ahead.

Zara typed into her arm comm to get the exact location of their medbay. "This way. The lab is underneath their medbay." She led the way down the packed streets.

I activated my arm comm to contact Honora. I didn't get a

response. She must have hers turned off. That didn't make me happy.

"No answer?" asked Alex.

"No," I said.

"Go into her head," he said.

"Copy that, but I need to be closer to do it. I'll contact her when we're at the medbay," I said as we dodged the pedestrians, rickshaws and hovercrafts on the street.

Zara picked up the pace. We arrived at city-center. A large glass building loomed to the left of the city park that had trees, a spacious lawn and an amusement park ride for kids.

We looked around. Everything looked calm. No police movements that we could see.

"If we find Anjori, then we could get a two-fer with rescuing Synthia too," said Stoller, putting a hand on his holstered gun.

"Honora's comm system is not on," I announced.

"Crap," said Zara.

"I can connect to her spinal sensor, but I need a minute," I explained.

"A minute is about all I'll give you," said Stoller as he looked around. I scanned his bio-levels. He was getting jumpy, and his nervous system was spiking. He was probably experiencing flashbacks or some kind of post-traumatic syndrome. I should have anticipated that. Stoller didn't seem to be the type of person who had led a trauma-free life. But then again, who had?

"You okay?" I asked.

"Yeah, yeah. Of course," said Stoller. He was lying. I would need to make it quick.

I closed my vision visor and closed all systems that weren't needed. In my mind, I formed my cube and sent a thought out to Honora. Nothing. Then she started to fade in.

Honora, where are you?

I'm in the planet-port with Meeor and Belin. I've hacked into their planet-port visitor gates. Just trying to find a sweet ride out of here. Where are you guys?

We're going into their medical facility. We received intel that Synthia and Anjori may be here.

Good, good. Is everyone fuming at me for taking off?

Yes.

I figured.

Send me your ship's registration name and number when you take off.

Will do, but later. Meeor told me there's a transport holding area for prisoners under the planet-port.

We heard that too. Second level.

Copy that. I'm going to try to rescue more Mawzians. All the ones we saw at the auction.

Good luck.

You too.

Honora faded from my cube. I brought the walls down and then got my systems back online.

"Okay, I'm back," I said as I turned to the team.

"How is she?' asked Alex.

"She's picking out the spaceship she will be taking," I said.

"You mean stealing. Great," said Zara.

"And she may be rescuing more Mawzians," I added, even though I knew they would hate hearing that latest update.

"Of course, she is," said Zara. "God, why does she have to be so good?"

"Look who's talking," said Stoller with a laugh.

Alex chuckled and then Zara smiled. "Yeah, can't fault her for rescuing people, friends or strangers."

"Let's check in Alex and get inside," said Stoller.

We crossed the park toward the medbay. There was limited security. Only two guards at the entrance. Not military soldiers or bots. The doors opened, and we approached the registration desk. A nurse greeted us. "How can I help you?"

Zara stepped up. "Our son scratched his arm, and I wanted to make sure it wasn't infected."

"I thought it was my leg," said Alex.

"It was your arm, son. Don't correct your mother," said Stoller.

The nurse looked at Zara, Alex and Stoller and smiled politely. "Whatever is scratched, the doctor can take a look at it. Young man, please follow me." The nurse turned around and headed for the back double doors.

The nurse turned around, surprised we were all following her. "Some of you can stay in the waiting area." She pointed to seating off to the side.

"We're good. We're a close family," said Stoller.

"Families that travel together, stay together," said Zara.

Stoller put his arm around Zara's waist. Zara grimaced and pushed his arm away.

"And your bot?" asked the nurse.

"Like family," said Alex. "It's been with us since I was born."

The nurse nodded and continued walking. She ushered us into a small med room. Real small. We squished in.

The nurse was not amused by all of us being in the patient's room. "Your doctor will be here shortly. Please fill out these forms." She handed a tablet to Zara. The nurse left.

Zara threw the tablet on the patient table. Stoller opened the door and peered out. "There's a closet at the end of the hall. I'll be right back."

"Let me see your leg," said Zara.

"What?" said Alex.

"Your leg," she repeated.

Alex lifted his leg and Zara pulled up his pants and scratched him deep with her nail.

"Ow!" yelled Alex.

"Just in case," said Zara.

"I thought we were going to say it was my arm?"

"No, we're back with the leg."

"I'm confused," said Alex as he looked down at his scratched leg.

There was a knock at the door.

"Sit," said Zara to Alex, who hopped onto the patient table.

The doctor walked in. He was surprised by my presence. I scanned him. His bio-levels were low. He was obviously tired and looked a bit out of sorts.

"So, how can I help you?" he asked Zara.

"My son scratched his leg. Just wanted to make sure it's not infected," said Zara.

Alex lifted his leg to reveal the recently made scratch. The doctor scanned it with his medstick. "Yes. Let me get some ointment for that. It should be a quick fix. Unless you prefer yaloites. They can get rid of any infection."

"What are yaloites?" asked Alex.

"Insects. Native to Mawzi. Found deep in our caverns. They are quite safe, I assure you. Unless they're hungry. We keep them well-fed at the clinic," said the doctor.

"Oh, no," said Alex.

"That will be fine. Thank you, doctor," said Zara.

The doctor smiled and shuffled out the door.

"I don't want any insects put on my leg, Zara," said Alex.

"I'm hoping that won't happen either, but you got to take one for the team, okay?" said Zara.

"I know, I just wish it didn't entail putting insects on the open sore that you gave me. Now I may really get an infection," snapped Alex.

"Not if you let the doc put yaloites on you," she snapped back. She got him on that one.

"Fine," he said as he sulked.

I was about to intervene when Stoller rushed in with four medical scrubs uniforms. He handed them out.

"This is the plan? Dress up as medical personnel?" asked Zara.

"Got a better one?" asked Stoller. "There's a stairwell in the back. We can take that down. But this is just for some temporary cover."

We started putting on the scrubs. Mine was tight. They all looked me over.

"Don't you have a human skin wrap?" asked Stoller.

"The Kells were making one for me, but I had to rush out of the lab the day the Heragi police arrested them," I explained.

"Here's a scrub cap. Keep your eyes down," said Stoller as he handed it to me. I put it on. From the looks on their faces, the cap didn't look so hot on me.

Stoller shrugged and then looked out the door again. "Let's go."

We filed out of the med room and headed down the hallway like we worked there. There were nurses in the hallway, but they didn't look toward us.

We reached the stairwell door and shuffled through it. I looked back and saw the doctor go into our patient room holding tweezers that had a twisting long black insect that must have been the yaloite. I was glad Alex didn't see it.

We dashed down the stairwell to the sub-fourth floor. We went into the hallway and located an empty equipment room.

"A floor below us, on the sub-fifth, is where those fly-boys said they conduct experiments," said Stoller. "I say we go in with weapons drawn."

"Okay, that's one approach," said Zara as she raised her eyebrows. "Alex, Gabe, do you have any other suggestions?"

Alex looked around and saw a gurney. "I agree but let's use this," he said as he pushed the gurney in front of us.

"Who's the patient?" asked Stoller.

"Gabe, of course," said Alex.

Of course. Great.

9

They wheeled me out of the equipment room with my body covered by a sheet and a breathing sensor covering my face. Stoller and Zara took the lead, rolling the gurney with Alex in the back near my head.

A few medical personnel passed by but didn't pay attention to us.

We came to a corner. Stoller peered around it. He turned back to us. "This is it. Two Heragi military-bots guarding a door."

"The fly-boys did say that Heragi officials have been negotiating with the Mawzians," said Zara.

"All pilots are great gossipers," said Stoller.

"Nice trait," said Zara dryly.

I tried to get up, but Stoller pushed me down. "No, Gabe. Our plan hasn't changed."

Did I mention that I didn't like this plan? Laying down doesn't exactly give me a good shot range from a tactical position.

"Ready?" asked Stoller.

"Always," said Zara.

"Yeah," said Alex.

"Affirmative," I muffled out from under the breathing sensor. My gurney began turning the corner. I leaned my head to the side to get a better view.

Stoller waved at the bots. "We have a new patient for Stefano. He ordered us to bring the patient down."

Stoller was a good actor. But I had figured that when we first met him at the Blue Edger bar.

The guard-bots put up their hands to stop him from reaching for the door handle.

"We need verification," said one of the guard-bots.

"I was ordered by Stefano to get this patient down to him before he expires. He just sent me a comm."

The second guard-bot sauntered around the gurney to take a look at me.

"Did he give you the pass phrase?" asked the guard-bot.

"Pass phrase?" said Stoller.

"Affirmative," said the guard-bot.

Stoller scratched his head like he was trying to remember a pass phrase. "Gosh, I have a bad memory. Let me think."

The second guard-bot started to pull back the sheet covering my body. I readied my gun.

Stoller kept looking back at the guard-bot near me. "Umm, how about—"

The guard-bot ripped the sheet off my body.

Stoller put his gun to the guard-bot's head. Zara ran up to the same guard-bot and put her finger on its off button at the back of his neck. "How about — Stefano is a creep." She pushed its off button, and the bot shut down.

"You're under—" the bot near me started. I pushed my gun into its face. I bolted up and grabbed the bot's gun.

"Arrest. Yeah, I know. Sorry, buddy," I said as I powered it down. It wasn't its fault it was made a guard-bot for a bad organization. It didn't have a choice.

We pushed the bots into a corner with their backs turned to

the wall, took off our scrubs and checked our weapons. Stoller nodded at us and busted through the door. I went in first with my weapon ready to fire.

Stefano spun around.

My eyes adjusted to three spotlights in the cavernous lab room.

On the left, in a wheelchair, was Synthia.

On the right, strapped onto a table that was tilted upward, was a woman, almost eight feet tall. I scanned her face, and it matched the Oliverian race. It had to be Anjori.

In the back were cots with a dozen or more Mawzians lying down. They were hooked to computers that lined the back wall.

Alex swept the room. There were no guard-bots inside the lab.

"How did you find me?" asked Stefano as he took off his glasses.

Zara ran to Synthia, who was catatonic. She kneeled down and touched Synthia's face. Synthia did not move.

Stoller approached Anjori. Her eyes were closed.

I marched up to Stefano and towered over him. He cowered in my shadow.

"We're asking the questions here, not you," I said.

Zara jumped up toward Stefano and pushed him into a chair.

Stoller paced back and forth in front of Anjori. He was hesitant to unleash her from the table she was strapped to. "Anjori," he whispered. "I came back. We're here to take you home, to Oliveria. Back to your sister. Back to your army."

Anjori lifted her eyelids halfway.

"She's alive, she's waking," shouted Stoller.

"Of course, she's alive. I never wanted to kill her. I'm not an idiot," said Stefano.

Zara hit him across the face with her gun.

"Oof," Stefano groaned. Blood ran down his cheek.

Zara looked back toward the Mawzians on the cots in the

back of the room. "What's going on over there?" She waved her weapon toward the Mawzians.

Alex ran to the back of the room and studied a few Mawzians and the computers they were hooked up to. "Their eyelids are moving back and forth. Just like Honora's did when she was operated on and Gabe's code was sequenced into her DNA."

"They're downloading code from the computer," said Zara as she ran to the back of the room.

Stefano smiled and wiped the blood dripping down his face.

"What did you do to the Mawzians?" I asked.

"The Mawzians? Just some enhancements," he said.

Zara took out her coder and connected to the computer console. "Hacking in," she shouted back to us.

"Anjori, wake up. It's Stoller."

Anjori tried to talk but no words came out. She pulled against her restraints.

Stoller turned to Stefano. "What'd you do to her?"

Stefano nodded to the back of the room. "Same as them," he said.

"And what exactly is that?" I asked.

Stefano looked up at me and smiled. "They're your children. Well, more like your siblings. Your cyborg siblings. Cybs," he said, and then he started laughing.

"What? What does he mean?" said Stoller.

"Shut down those computers, Zara," said Alex.

"I can't. I mean, I don't know what will happen if I shut them down. It could kill them all," she said, looking over her coder.

"Ooh, what a dilemma," said Stefano with a cackle.

Zara strode up to Stefano and hit him again, now with her coder.

Another stream of blood emerged from Stefano's mouth. He smiled with bloody teeth. "Killing a bot is one thing, but killing something organic is quite another, isn't it?"

I moved Zara away from Stefano.

"You took code from Honora and Talia," I said.

"You enhanced the Mawzians with it, correct?" asked Zara.

"That is why I hired you back on Suissey. You're so quick," said Stefano. "Maybe too quick for your own good."

I sensed footsteps running down the hallway toward us. I turned to cover the door. "We got incoming," I shouted. I braced myself and pulled out my weapon.

Alex came running up from the back of the lab.

Stoller put himself in front of Anjori. Zara crouched in front of Synthia to protect her.

A unit of Heragi guard-bots plunged into the room. The guard-bots we had turned off in the hallway must have alerted their security system before they powered down.

"Intruders! Kill them!" yelled Stefano.

I opened fire, followed by Stoller, Zara and Alex. Guard-bots fell and those that escaped our laser shots used their fallen colleague bots as cover.

A bot was thrown at Stoller and it knocked him down. Another bot fired at him, and he rolled to his side and hit the bot with a shot to the chest.

One bot was charging me using a dead bot as a shield. Zara had a clear side shot and knocked it out.

I shot two bots that were coming down hard on Alex who was knocked to the ground. He was hit on his right leg. He yelled in pain. I ran over to him. His wound wasn't too bad.

All the Heragi bots were down.

"Let's get out of here," shouted Stoller as he began to untie Anjori from her table. She crumpled to the ground.

Zara whispered into Synthia's ear, trying to wake her up.

"What do we do with the Mawzians?" asked Alex.

"We can't take them. We have no time," I said.

"Gabe's right," Zara said.

"But they're cyborgs with my sister's and Gabe's code," said Alex.

"Yes, that's right, boy, you understand. They're like family now," said Stefano as he crawled toward Alex.

"We may not be able to take them, but we're definitely taking *you* with us," said Zara.

Synthia was waking. "Zara, always rescuing me."

"Yeah, I need to put a tracker on you," said Zara. "Can you walk?"

"Yes, somewhat," she said.

"I'll help you," said Zara as she put her arm around Synthia.

I yanked Stefano out of his chair and pushed him in front of me.

"How's Anjori?" asked Alex as he limped over to her.

Stoller had pushed Anjori to a sitting position with her back against the upright table. "I don't know."

He leaned over her. "Time to go, Anjori."

Her arm flew out and grabbed Stoller's shoulder. "Don't leave me," she said.

"I won't. I promise. But we first have to get out of this building and back to the ship," he said. "Can you get up?"

She grimaced and got to her knees. With a grunt, she heaved her large frame upward. She was in pain. She headed toward the door and then turned around. She made a straight line to the computers that were hooked up to the Mawzians.

"No!" yelled Stefano.

Anjori pulled all the connection lines from the Mawzian test subjects to the computers and shut down the whole system. I scanned the Mawzians' bio-metrics. All their bodily functions were failing rapidly.

"She's killing them," whispered Alex.

Zara looked away.

None of us tried to stop her.

"That's why she's a general," said Stoller in a hushed tone.

Anjori limped back to us. She looked at Alex. "Let's go."

We gathered ourselves and checked our weapons. Anjori

grabbed two bot guns from the floor. She was formidable in her size and grit. A tattered Oliverian uniform hung on her lean frame. She took a glance at me. "Whose bot?"

"No one's. He's with us. He's our captain," Stoller responded.

"My name is Gabe."

She looked me up and down. "Lead the way."

I put my hand on Stefano and pushed him ahead of me, using him like a shield.

We headed toward the elevator and all pushed inside.

"We'll need a bigger ship," joked Stoller.

"Yeah, or a second one," said Alex.

"Thank goodness Honora can pilot a ship," said Zara.

I checked the bio-metrics of Synthia and Anjori while in the elevator. Synthia was in bad shape. All her vitals were down. Anjori's system was suppressed but quickly recovering. In fact, she was getting stronger by the second.

The elevator doors opened.

We ran down the back office of the medbay where we were earlier roomed. The doctor who was helping us saw our team, and he started yelling, "Guards, get the guards. Alert security!"

I pushed the doctor through an open medbay door and closed it.

Nurses scattered in the hallway.

We hiked through the entry doors to the admitting area. I was about to take point to get us out of the building when Anjori took the lead. She scanned the perimeter and aimed at Heragi guard-bots and Mawzians who tried to stop our exit from the medical building. Every shot she released was on target. She was fast, real fast, on the gun draw.

Zara helped Synthia walk. Stoller ran in front of Anjori. "We need to cross over the park and get down into a service tunnel."

Anjori nodded as she continued to fire rounds at guards that approached us. They had no chance against her.

I glanced over to Alex and noticed he was faltering. I put my arm around him to help him run.

We ran out of the medical building and crossed over the city center park. Mawzians and visitors scattered when they saw us running with brandished weapons. Stoller guided us down the streets until we passed the Swift Zuri bar we had stopped at earlier.

The two pilots, Jablo and Nei, crept out with their guns extended. "Looks like you found the med building," said Jablo.

"I knew there was something off about you folks," said Nei.

"We did. Thanks to you. And we are a bit off. All of us," said Stoller as he shot Jablo in the leg.

Anjori took out the leg of his partner Nei.

They both dropped their weapons and writhed on the ground screaming. We walked over them.

Stoller found the ladder that led to the service tunnel. Synthia needed extra help descending. We reached the tunnel. Anjori was so tall she had to duck.

"This way," said Stoller.

I punched my arm comm to get a link to Honora.

No answer. I waited.

"Gabe, I'm here," Honora responded.

"Where is here?" I asked.

"I'm at the planet-port. Lifting off now. I've got to go. Taking heavy fire," she said. Then her comm went dead.

Blasted. I hated leaving her alone.

"She's got your pilot skills. She's got your code," said Synthia to reassure me about Honora's capacity to take care of herself.

"Let's go, Gabe," said Alex. "I wish I was with her, too."

We hustled across the vast rooms and ran past the large cathedral down to the narrowing tunnel. We came to an airlock room.

Stoller and I opened our backpacks to get the two extra suits.

He gave one to Zara to help Synthia suit up. "I don't have enough suits," he said in a flat tone.

"Give that one to Stefano. I'll wait," said Anjori.

"I'll run back with one for Anjori," I said.

"Okay," said Stoller. "I'm not coming back a third time." He laughed to cut the tension.

Everyone suited up but Anjori. We had to leave her in the hallway before the airlock chamber. We entered the chamber and depressurized the room. The next door opened up to the tunnel with the entrance lid above to the planet surface.

I would need to open it on my own without Honora's help this time.

I jumped up and tried to push up on the lid, leveraging my legs off a wall. The lid was too heavy. Then I saw Alex raise his hands. The lid starting moving. He was using his mind to move it. I pushed harder and the lid moved off to the side.

"Thanks," I said to Alex. "Why didn't you help last time?"

"You and Honora were handling it," he said.

He was correct. Technically.

The team climbed up the utility ladder, and I helped them outside. I left the lid slightly cracked open, knowing I was coming back. Red sand was being sucked down into the tunnel. The pressure leakage would soon send out a warning signal to the Mawzian security system. I needed to return quickly with a suit for Anjori.

"Feti," I shouted into my arm comm. "Begin launch procedures."

"Copy that, Gabe," Feti replied.

Zara grabbed Synthia's shoulder and led her to our ship. Stoller helped Alex, and we hustled as fast as we could to the *Alyssia*. The ramp lowered, and we scrambled up it. I grabbed another large atmospheric suit, which may still not be big enough for Anjori.

"Good luck," yelled Stoller as I ran down the ramp.

I looked off toward the planet-port and saw two Heragi naval ships rising up and attacking a commercial ship. That must be Honora. I ran faster up the red hill to the tunnel lid.

With all my strength, I pulled up on the lid and dropped down into the tunnel, skipping the ladder. I landed on the growing mound of sand falling in from the surface and ran into the airlock chamber. After pressurizing the door, it opened to Anjori. She was crouched, firing down the tunnel at Mawzians. She jumped into the airlock chamber, and I closed the door.

I handed the suit to Anjori. She took one look at it and threw it to the ground. "This suit won't fit, only the helmet," she said. "I'll have to do without it."

"You'll only have ten seconds before the radiation poisoning begins," I said.

"I get it," she said. "Better than staying here another day."

I nodded and depressurized the airlock. The door opened, and we went to the ladder. Anjori crouched, and in one giant leap, she jumped up, clearing the opening. I copied her and made the same leap. I hit the sand and saw she was already in full sprint toward the *Alyssia*.

I counted as I followed her at my maximum speed. One, Two, Three, Four.

She was down the side of the hill.

Five, Six, Seven, Eight.

She faltered and fell right before the ramp.

I came up behind her and pulled up her arm. She got to her feet.

Nine. Her feet hit the ramp.

Ten. She was halfway up.

Eleven. She dove into the spaceship. I was right behind and hit the ramp closure. It reeled up.

Twelve. It was closed.

She was on the ground in the airlock chamber. I pressurized the room. I bent down and turned her over. Her face was red. Radiation sores were forming.

"You're inside me," she whispered right before she passed out.

The airlock door opened, and Stoller rushed in.

"Don't touch her," I yelled. I picked up Anjori and took her to medbay.

I laid Anjori on the surgical table. The same table that we used when we operated on Honora during our last mission. Blasted. Honora. Where was she?

Zara, Synthia and Stoller followed me into the medbay.

"You'll need to treat her for radiation poisoning," I said as I left the room. I had to get us out of here and help Honora.

I ran down to the bridge and saw that Alex was already strapped into the port turret. Goggins was at his navigation console.

"Dr. Goggins," I said, acknowledging him.

"Nice to see you, Gabe," he said with a calmness I hadn't heard before in his voice. He must be getting used to these missions.

"Ready, Alex?" I yelled.

"Ready, Gabe," Alex yelled back.

"Let's give Honora cover."

"Copy that," said Alex.

I turned and saw Talia strapped in her seat with her cici-chimp. She gave me a thumbs up sign. I gave her a thumbs up back. At least I knew Talia and Alex were okay.

I opened up the ship's comms. "Hold on, everyone. Feti, we're lifting off in three, two, one."

"Affirmative, Gabe. Lifting off," it said.

We rose off the red dirt of Mawzi, and I turned the *Alyssia* toward the planet-port. I saw Honora's ship ahead of us.

"Feti, please get us a comm link to that commercial ship ahead."

"Connecting, Gabe," said Feti.

I raced us over to the airfight that Honora was having with two Heragi naval ships.

"Go ahead, Gabe," said Feti.

"Honora, it's Gabe," I said as I spun the *Alyssia* around to be in range of the two Heragi ships.

"Hey, there. Nice to see you," she said with a bit of strain in her voice. "Mind taking on one of these jerks?"

"Sure," I said as I moved closer to give Alex a clean shot.

"Firing," yelled Alex. He opened up on the Heragi ships. He severely damaged their bridge. The Heragi ship fired back, and we took a hit on our port side below where Alex sat. Our damage was recoverable. I spun around again and took a look at Honora's progress.

She fired a missile toward the Heragi ship she was battling. The pilots ejected, and the ship broke up and blew up. Pieces of the ship headed toward one of the smaller Mawzi domes.

"Blasted," she said. "I didn't want it to go down on a dome."

The ship hit the dome but broke up into smaller pieces upon impact. There may have been damage to the dome, but it did not crack wide open. Thank goodness.

I looked back to the remaining Heragi ship and readied our missile system. I led the naval ship out farther over the red desert. One of their missiles was locked onto us. I maneuvered away and released two drones, acting as countermeasures to pull their missiles away from us. Their missiles were approaching the *Alyssia*.

"Gabe, their missiles are too close," yelled Goggins.

"Let the drones do their job," I said.

They better do their job.

The Heragi missiles peeled away and followed the drones. The missiles exploded in the red sky.

"That was too close for comfort," sighed Goggins.

"I agree, Dr. Goggins." I turned around and fired upon the ship. Direct hit. It exploded over the desert. "Follow me, Honora."

"Copy that."

We flew out of the Mawzi atmosphere into space. The bridge window view darkened, and we could see the surrounding moons, planets and stars.

"Goggins, get us on the Karakova Highway, please," I said.

"You got it, Gabe." Goggins punched in the coordinates.

It felt good to be in space.

I looked back at Talia. She sent me a thought. *You found Anjori.*

Yes.

She's tall.

Yes, she is.

She's different.

She is now.

Because of Stefano. Does she have our DNA?

Yes.

Then she's family.

I guess she is. She killed Mawzians who also had our DNA. She didn't blink an eye.

Talia looked out her window. I wasn't sure if I should've told her about what Anjori did, but she would have learned about it from Alex.

Talia?

Was there another option?

There always is, but I think she was right.

We each must answer for our actions. I need to meditate now for the Mawzians.

Turning back toward my console, pain stabbed my chest.

I looked into my monitoring screens to see Honora's ship following us. I relaxed into my seat, waiting for us to approach the Karakova Highway.

99

10

I navigated us onto the Karakova Highway, and Honora followed in her pirated ship with twenty rescued Mawzians. What were we going to do with those rescued? I didn't want to think about that right now. I needed to talk with the crew about where we were headed next.

I gave Feti control of the ship. Goggins tracked our mapping progress and chatted with Honora over comms. "You're as stubborn as your mother," said Goggins.

I passed him, and he pointed to his comms unit and rolled his eyes. I touched his shoulder. I was glad he and Honora were getting along so well. Like that was ever going to happen, but it was nice to hear them trying.

I sat down next to Talia, who was looking off into space. She turned to me, and I sent her a thought. *Do you want to come with me to check on Synthia?*

She nodded. *Yes.*

Synthia rested on one of the beds in medbay. Talia hugged her and held her hand.

I scanned Synthia's bio-metrics. She was doing better. Her eyes opened when I was looking over her, and she grabbed my hand. She sent me a thought. *Gabe, thank you.*

You're welcome. What was Stefano having you do? I didn't see any rebel prisoners in the basement.

He didn't have me there to see if any prisoners were lying.

Then what?

He had me there to test his prisoners' telepathic gifts.

Stoller entered medbay. "I have Stefano locked up in one of the personal quarters." He headed over to Anjori who was receiving medicine to counteract her radiation poisoning. Her eyes were shut.

Alex was on another bed being tended to by Zara. He winced as she sprayed disinfectant on his leg wound.

"Stop flinching," she chastised him.

"It hurts," he said.

"I should have grabbed some of those yaloites before we left," she said with a smirk.

Alex laughed. "I'd rather take the pain."

I walked over to Alex as Zara finished wrapping up his leg. "Another fine job you did, Alex," I said.

"Thanks, Gabe. Are you mad at Honora for rescuing those Mawzians?"

"No, I can't seem to stay mad at any of you," I said, and I meant it.

He smiled and then yelled, "Ow, not so tight, Zara." Which made her wrap the bandage tighter for a moment before she loosened it.

"There, is that better?" She tousled his hair.

"Yes, thank you."

I crossed to Anjori's table. She was talking softly to Stoller. Zara joined us.

Her bio-metrics came up in my visor, showing her radiation

levels were coming down. She was recovering but may have permanent radiation damage.

Talia and Gabe helped guide Synthia over to Anjori. They all wanted to view the woman warrior.

Anjori looked up to me. "Thank you."

"You're welcome," I said.

"What are you?" she asked.

"I'm a robot, built with rogue code by my creators," I said.

"For what purpose?"

"Ava and Damiel Kell built me to protect their children and to take them off the planet Heragi. To do that, they wrote code that gave me the ability to kill humans — at my discretion — at any time," I explained.

"But there's more to you," said Anjori.

"I can be programmed to be mission directed. I have advanced pilot and combat programs, alien languages, anything that can aid in a battle. And telepathic communication."

"More," she said.

"I feel pain," I said.

"Why?"

"Ava and Damiel said I needed to feel pain to be empathetic. Ava wanted me to feel to be protective of her children. So that I would bond with them. It's part of my sentient program," I said.

"You're evolving," she said.

"Yes, my code is mutating," I said.

"You are more than when you left the lab," said Zara.

"Yes," I said.

"What did Stefano do to you, Anjori?" asked Stoller.

"I don't know exactly. When he arrived with Synthia, he set up the lab. Prior to that, I was left alone by the Mawzians. Ten years of being alone. I almost looked forward to it when Stefano first arrived. At least someone would talk to me," she said.

"Synthia, fill in the gaps for us," said Zara.

"He's mixing up all the code. DNA code from the Kell children and Gabe's code," said Synthia.

"How come he didn't use your DNA?" asked Stoller.

"I'm not a humanoid. My people are from the planet Ellium. He tried that back on Suissey," Synthia explained.

"And what is the end game?" asked Stoller.

"Just what Stefano said in the lab. Those Mawzians were enhanced. He made them cyborgs. Half human, half robot. Sentient robots, like Gabe. But Stefano gave them code instructions to kill against their own will. They have a prime directive to kill enemies of the Heragi Empire," Synthia explained.

"I had to kill them," said Anjori.

"I couldn't do it," said Zara.

"They were a threat," said Anjori. "Come to think of it, you should have killed me." There was pain in her eyes.

Stoller backed away from the table. "I didn't risk my life for the second time to just off you, Anjori. Why are you so frightened? I don't ever remember you being that way before."

Synthia stepped forward.

"You didn't see the first ones. The beginning of his experiments. It took him time to perfect the coding. They died horrible deaths," said Synthia.

"And they followed his horrible orders," said Anjori as she pushed herself up to a sitting position. "He had them fight each other, to see if they would obey his directions. I also had to fight them."

Talia put her hands to her mouth. She shook her head. Alex put his arm around his sister to comfort her.

I'm sorry, Talia's transceiver stated loudly. *I'm so sorry.*

"This isn't your fault, Talia. Jakawa and Stefano took your and Honora's DNA. We just need to deal with it," said Zara.

"There was a man named Foxwell," said Anjori. "He was there, too, on the first day. He was giving orders to Stefano. They were huddled over looking at the first Mawzians they tested. It was his idea to have them fight each other. If I ever get near him again, I will put a quiet end to him."

"Now that's the Anjori I remember," said an enthused Stoller as he made his hands into fists and stepped toward her.

"You tried to rescue me before?"

"Five years ago."

"They never told me."

"Sorry it took me so long to get back," he said.

"What about my family? My sister?" she asked.

"I haven't been in contact with them. Except your nephew Tristan. I was so ashamed that I left my position. I failed them and you," confessed Stoller.

"You came back, that's all that matters," said Anjori.

"The only reason I came back is because I met these people who knew Synthia was on Mawzi. I'm not that chivalrous," he confessed.

"Then it was meant to be. Timing and the universe colluded."

They were good with each other. I was glad Anjori could forgive him. She had ten years to contemplate many things, including forgiveness.

"We need to interrogate Stefano," I whispered to Stoller.

He nodded.

"I'll get him," I said.

I entered the hallway to the personal cabinet quarters and tapped on my arm comm.

"Feti, can you open this cabinet door?"

"Yes, Gabe. Is everything all right? Who's your prisoner?" it asked.

"Just a man," I said. "A bad man."

"Did he hurt that tall woman we picked up?"

"Yes, and Synthia too," I replied.

"I don't like bad men. Mr. Gates is a bad man," said Feti about the *Alyssia*'s former owner and his former boss.

"We'll try to keep the bad men quota to a minimum on the *Alyssia* from now on, okay?"

"Sounds good. Thank you, Gabe. Opening the door now," said Feti.

"Thank you, Feti," I said.

Stefano was lying down on the bunk. He was singing to himself. He looked up. "Are you going to sucker punch me again?" he asked, referring to the right hook I gave him back on Zaradorba when he had kidnapped Honora and Talia.

"Not yet," I replied. "Get up. We're going to have a talk."

"What if I don't feel like talking?"

"Then we can have Synthia go into your mind. That would be fair, wouldn't it? You made her break into so many minds of others that I'm sure she would like to poke around in yours."

"Why not Talia?"

I loomed over him. "No, keep away from her."

"Family, huh?"

I didn't reply.

"The Kells did some wonderful coding on you, and it came in quite handy when working on the cybs."

I picked him up off the bed and dumped him on his feet. "Let's go."

With a hard push, I sent Stefano crashing into a medbay chair. Stoller stepped forward to begin the questioning.

"Gabe, we shouldn't have him in here with Anjori," warned Synthia as soon as she saw Stefano.

Stoller stepped forward in front of Stefano, ignoring Synthia. "We understand you took the Kell kids' and Gabe's code, mixed it up and shot it into the Mawzians and Anjori."

"Sounds about right," answered Stefano, tapping his fingers

on his lap. He was excited. His bio-levels were rising, not in fear but excitement. I hated this guy.

"What were you planning to do with the Mawzians?" asked Zara.

"Not were — *are*," replied Stefano with a smile. "Anjori or Synthia must have filled you in. Didn't they overhear the conversations Foxwell and I had in the lab? You saw it for yourself. We're making a cyborg army with Gabe's rogue code and the Kell children's DNA with all the ancient gifts they possess," explained Stefano. He slapped his hands on his lap faster.

He was downright giddy.

"Please, Gabe, listen to me. Get him out of the room," pleaded Synthia.

I tried to soothe Synthia. "It will be all right."

"And you know what?" He stopped and looked around. "It worked. It really worked. Didn't it, Synthia? Didn't it, Anjori?"

"It did," said Synthia in a hush tone.

"You're lucky I'm not alone with you," seethed Anjori.

"Would you like to see a demonstration?" asked Stefano with a grin. No one answered. "Come on, you guys are no fun." He looked around the room. "Zara, you appreciate good coding. Don't you want to see what I created?"

"No," she said as she backed away from him.

"Alex? Talia? Would you like to see what I did with your DNA? You see, part of you is inside Anjori. You're kind of related. Like siblings. Isn't that cool? Isn't that neat?"

Talia was getting frightened. Alex pulled Talia behind him and backed away.

"Stop him," yelled Synthia.

"Alex, get Talia out of here," I ordered. Alex grabbed Talia and led her out of the medbay.

"Let's do a test run, Anjori, shall we?" asked Stefano.

"No." Anjori stood up. She towered over everyone in the room. I looked up at her and then over to Stefano. He was going to trigger her like the Kells triggered and launched my mission. I lunged for Stefano.

"*Kogeki!*" yelled Stefano.

My right fist came down on Stefano's cheek and knocked him to the ground unconscious. I turned around to Anjori.

Stoller didn't understand what was happening. "Gabe?"

"Anjori, whatever directories are opening, try to stop them," I ordered.

Anjori backed up. A frightened look crossed her face. She closed her eyes and grabbed her head. "I can't stop it," she whined.

"Gabe, what is happening?" asked Stoller.

Anjori screamed.

Zara grabbed Synthia, who was groaning. "No, no." She pulled Synthia to the back of the room.

"You can control it, Anjori. You must try," I said as I pulled out my gun.

When Stoller saw me pull the gun on Anjori, he pulled his gun out and pointed it at me. "Gabe, what in the galaxy are you doing? Put your gun down."

"Zara, get your coder out," I said.

At that moment, Goggins came in, chatting with Honora on his arm comm. "Hey, what's the hold up? I've got Honora here. We need to figure out what to do with the Mawzians." He looked around and saw my and Stoller's guns drawn. He dropped his arm comm to the floor.

I heard Honora's voice on the other end of his comm device. "Hello? Goggins? Gabe? What's going on?"

Stefano came to and pulled himself up to his knees. He looked at Goggins' arm comm and dove for it. "Kogeki, my lovely Mawzians. Kogeki!" Stefano screamed into the comm.

I lunged for him and knocked the comm device out of his hands.

"What? Who was that? Is that Stefano?" yelled Honora.

I slugged Stefano as hard as I could which knocked him across the floor.

Anjori pounded her head into a nearby surgical tray. She was trying to control her mind, but she wasn't succeeding.

"Anjori? Stop, you're hurting yourself," said Stoller.

"Stoller, get away. Everyone, out of the room," I screamed. "A mission directory is downloading into her brain. It's a prime directive from Stefano and Foxwell. Just like the Kells gave me a mission."

"She can't stop it," said Synthia. "None of them could. None of the Mawzians. They tore each other apart."

Why would Stefano yell into Goggin's comm device?

Then it hit me.

"Synthia, were there more Mawzian slaves transformed into cybs?"

She rubbed her head and strained to think back. "There could have been. Some came and went. Some lived, some died. Maybe ten or…"

"Twenty," I said, finishing her sentence. The twenty that were on Honora's ship. It was happening to them too. And Honora was all alone.

Anjori straightened herself out and came to attention like a soldier. She looked down at Stoller with coldness. "Eliminate all enemies of the Heragi Empire," she said in a monotone voice as she scanned the room. "Five."

Five? I looked around the room. Me, Stoller, Zara, Goggins and Synthia.

Anjori heaved her left arm at Stoller, knocking him across the room.

"Go!" I yelled at the others. Zara and Goggins helped Synthia, and they all ran out of the medbay. Stoller was stunned. He crawled on the ground like a crab, backing away.

"Anjori, it's Stoller. Stop this," he yelled at her.

Her pupils moved in rapid motion left and right. Code crossed them. More files were opening and forming directories in her brain. All of my pilot and combat directories. And the children's gifts, telepathy, healing and telekinesis. Her knowledge and power quadrupled in seconds before our eyes.

Stefano laughed as he looked into Anjori's eyes that now had his latest code running across them.

"She's gone, Stoller. Take Stefano. Head to the stern. Arm up," I said.

Stoller grabbed Stefano and dragged him out.

Screaming came from Goggins' arm comm on the floor near me. I grabbed it. "Honora?"

"Gabe, something's happening to the Mawzians. They're in pain. I don't know what to do."

"Kill them. You need to kill them all," I said.

Anjori marched toward me.

"What? No, I won't do that," said Honora.

"They have a prime directive that makes them killers. They will kill all enemies of the Empire. They're going to come after you in seconds."

I heard more Mawzian screams, and then her comm went dead.

Anjori was right over me now.

We looked into each other's eyes.

I fired my gun at her legs. She let out a grunt as she fell to the ground. She looked at her wound and put her left hand on her damaged leg and closed her eyes. She was concentrating. Her leg began to heal. She could self-heal. That came from Honora's DNA.

I got on my feet and backed away out the door.

"Feti, close and lock the medbay," I yelled.

The door closed and locked.

"Copy that, Gabe. Closed and locked," it said.

I backed into the hallway wall. Anjori pounded on the door over and over. I ran down the hall with Anjori's pounding echoing behind me.

11

Stoller was arming up when I got to the equipment room. He threw me a gun and then gave me another.

"Put them on stun phase," he ordered. I did what he said although I didn't think that would be effective.

"She can self-heal," I said. "Stun won't be enough."

"Do it!" yelled Stoller. I didn't have to scan his bio-metrics to know he was stressed and conflicted on who the enemy was and what he would need to do to his old friend. I reviewed scenario probabilities. This wasn't going to end well for anyone.

"Where is she?" he growled.

"Locked in the medbay," I said. "I'm not sure how long the door will hold."

"We're not killing her," he said. "We just need to subdue her until we can figure this all out."

I needed to let him think that, at least for now. I didn't want to kill Anjori either. But if it came down to her or us, my only choice would be us. I hoped Stoller felt the same way. I may not be his first choice to save if he had to choose between me and Anjori, even if she was now a cyborg.

"Copy that," I said.

We hustled out of the equipment room back to the medbay and opened up a comm to the bridge.

"Zara, Goggins, any luck on a comm link to Honora?" I asked.

"No, none," he said,

"Okay, keep an eye on her ship."

"Affirmative, Gabe. No change in their course," said Goggins.

"How's our situation?" asked Zara.

"Anjori is locked in the medbay. Are the kids on the bridge?"

"Yes, everyone is here except you and Stoller. We even have dirtbag Stefano here. And he won't wipe that smile off his face. Permission to strike him?" asked Zara.

"That would be a no. Keep working with Feti to get a comms link to Honora's ship," I said. "Goggins, you and Feti figure out a docking procedure with that ship. We need to get inside pronto," I said.

"Copy that," replied Goggins.

"Will do, Gabe," said Zara. "We'll keep interrogating Stefano. Maybe there's a way to reverse the coding or change the prime directive he inserted in them."

"Copy that," I said.

I didn't feel hopeful about Zara being able to figure out how to reverse the cyborg effect that Stefano had created. At least in the short term.

As Stoller and I approached the medbay, the air vibrated from continuous beating on the door. We came up to the door, and it stopped.

I glanced at Stoller. His face was full of dread.

"Anjori? Anjori?" he yelled. "Maybe we can talk her out of this," he whispered to me.

I nodded but didn't think that was possible. Sometimes you have to let humans fail.

Stoller stepped closer to the door. "We know you don't want

to hurt us, and it's just some crazy prime directive that Stefano put in you."

Silence.

"I know you. You don't kill innocent people," he continued as he turned to me.

A terrific crash hit the door. Anjori had pushed a gurney right through the door, and it busted open. Stoller and I were knocked down.

Anjori appeared in the doorway. She stepped over the fallen door and picked up Stoller by the scruff of his shirt. He struggled as she lifted him off his feet. With barely a twitch of her bicep, she slammed him into the adjacent wall. "You are not innocent," she said.

She tightened her grip around his neck.

I took out my gun and fired a stun shot. She dropped Stoller and doubled over. Her recovery was quick, and she turned on me. I backed up.

There was no reasoning with her. She, or it, wasn't Anjori at this point.

"Stoller, I'm turning my gun to kill phase," I said.

"No!" he yelled. He found his gun on the ground and fired into Anjori's back. She faltered but kept coming for me. I kept backing up. He shot her again. And again. Her strength was undeniable.

I hadn't turned my gun to kill phase yet. I wasn't sure how long I could hold off.

The airlock.

I would lead her to the airlock.

As I was backing up down the hallway, Stoller kept firing at Anjori, only temporarily slowing her. We arrived at the airlock chamber door, and I opened it.

"What are you doing?" yelled Stoller.

I backed all the way into the chamber and put my back against the door leading out to space. The chamber seal was fortified, and the door was the sturdiest one on the ship. If I could lead her there, it was the best place to hold her, and the easiest place to space her, as in, open the exterior door and have her pulled out into the Edge.

Anjori turned and hit Stoller with a left hook that sent him flying into the wall. He groaned and tried to get to his feet, but the blow was too staggering. He faltered. It was just me and her.

She ran into the chamber and came straight in for an attack. She punched my face and then my chest.

I doubled over, and she knocked me to my knees, causing me to lose the grip on my gun. She put her hands around my neck. She was trying to tear my head off. I searched for my gun on the ground. My pain thresholds skyrocketed. My fingers touched the gun and I grabbed it. I flicked the phase button to kill and pulled it up to her head. She stopped.

She had a self-preservation directive in her program. Anjori pulled her hands off my neck.

I backed out of the room and shut the airlock chamber door, locking Anjori in it.

Alex ran down the hallway and helped Stoller to his feet. I glanced back at Anjori through the chamber window, and her warrior face was stern.

"Why did she stop?" asked Alex.

"Unlike me, she has self-preservation code," I said.

She began hitting the chamber door with both arms. That was one angry cyborg.

Stoller turned from the door window and leaned against the wall. He couldn't watch her like this anymore. I imagined it must be hard, but I had no history with Anjori, and she had tried to kill me now, twice.

"Gabe, we need to get Honora, now," Alex said as he ran to the suit room.

"Any comms?" I asked as Stoller and I followed him.

"No, we need to board her ship. We can use the back door hatch to send a bridge to Honora's ship."

"Wait, hold it. We're on the Karakova Highway. That's insane to try to connect to a ship on this highway. Our speed makes it too risky," reasoned Stoller as he put his hand on Alex's spacesuit. Alex yanked it away.

"That's my sister on that ship. All alone with a bunch of raving cyborgs trying to kill her," Alex shouted.

"Wait. Let me try to connect to her in her mind," I said.

"Talia and Synthia tried that, Gabe. They couldn't connect," Alex said.

"The highway harmonics may be interfering," said Stoller.

I closed down my vision and went into my mind. I built my cube and called out Honora's name. I waited for her to appear. Nothing. Then she faded in but only partially. Stoller was right. The highway harmonics were interfering. She was hazy, but I could make her out. Her hands were outstretched. She was wearing a spacesuit. Then she was gone. I struck down my cube and opened my eyes.

"I saw her. She had on a spacesuit," I said.

Goggins came over the ship's comm. "Gabe, the airlock door is opening on Honora's ship."

Stoller, Alex and I ran to the nearest window. Freighters and private ships passed by us. Honora's access door was opening. One figure in a spacesuit stood near the door.

"It's Honora," whispered Alex.

"That's suicide. She can't jump out onto the highway," replied Stoller. "The g-force is ridiculous."

"She just did," I said as we watched Honora hurl her body out into space. She tumbled over and over, barely missing being hit. She tried to straighten herself with the small nitrogen jet thrusters on her suit.

"I'm going after her," I said.

"No, she's my sister. I'm going. I don't have to pull a gun on you, do I, Gabe? We Kells are stubborn," said Alex as he touched his gun.

"You certainly are. Fine, suit up. We need to guide her in." I ran toward the bridge.

I jumped into my commander seat and took control of the ship from Feti.

"Gabe, Honora just jumped —" started Goggins.

"I know, we saw her," I said.

"The highway harmonics are keeping her speed constant with ours," he said as he put his fingers through his hair. "How is that possible?"

"Stoller said this highway is of a higher intelligence," said Synthia. "I believe they're helping her."

"I hope they keep helping her. Feti, connect my comm to the whole ship, Alex's suit, and try to connect to Honora out there," I asked.

"Copy that, Gabe. You're coming through the ship's comm and Alex's suit. Having trouble linking to Honora's suit though," it said.

"Keep trying," I instructed.

I attempted to slow our speed, but the highway was in control of that. I tried different maneuvers and started slowly reversing the engines.

"Gabe, reversing engines puts the ship in jeopardy of breaking up. Please cease," Feti warned.

"Need to do it, Feti. We need to reach Honora," I said.

"This is not optimal," it said.

"I agree. It never is," I said. "But I'm doing it anyway. Where is she, Goggins?"

He looked on his monitor and then pointed out the window. I glanced out along with Zara, Synthia and Talia. "Behind us, on our starboard. Reversing the engines is helping, but our fellow travelers on the highway are not happy."

Ships dodged away from Honora and weaved out and then in front of us as we slowed down.

"I'm sure they're all giving us their middle finger if they have one," commented Zara.

"Gabe, look. Alex is being extended out with a line," said Goggins.

"Brave kid," whispered Zara.

I glanced over to Talia. She had her face pressed against a window.

He'll get her, was the thought I sent to Talia.

She couldn't kill them, Talia thought.

Apparently not, I thought. *Can you try to connect with her again?*

Talia closed her eyes. *She's scared. She's not able to speak.*

Honora probably needed all her concentration to control her spin in space.

"How are we doing, Goggins?" I asked.

"Good. I mean, as well as we can," he replied. "Alex is almost to her."

"Alex, talk to me," I said.

In a few seconds, he came over the comm. "I'm getting closer. I need more extension. Stoller, give me the whole wire."

Stoller's voice came over the comms. "Almost at the end of your line, kid."

"Honora, Honora," Alex called to his sister.

"Zara, any help you can give Feti on Honora's comms?" I asked.

Zara was already working on it. She pounded on her console. "Got her. Go ahead now, Alex."

"Copy that. Honora? I'm coming for you," said Alex. His voice was strained. Ships were dodging them both now. It should have been me out there, not Alex. Ava would never forgive me for this one.

Honora's voice broke into the comm. "I'm trying." She finally got control of her spin and exhaled. "Got it," she said with relief.

They both pushed their thrusters to get closer. Alex reached out both hands and so did Honora.

Goggins focused on his console. "Twenty yards, fifteen, ten, five —" He stopped.

Alex grabbed Honora as she almost flew past him.

"Gotcha," Alex yelled as he latched his external line to her. "She's secure. Reel us in!"

"He has her!" yelled Goggins. "Thank goodness."

I agreed with Goggins. Thank goodness.

Synthia hugged Talia.

Zara sighed with relief. "Thank the universe."

"Thank the higher intelligence of the highway," said Synthia.

"Even I would agree with you on that one, Synthia," said Goggins. "That defies what I was taught at University."

"There is much our universe could teach the universities," quipped Synthia.

Goggins looked over to her and nodded in agreement. "I bet there is."

"How are they doing, Stoller?" I called.

"They're doing okay. Reeling them both in now," he said into his comm at the back of the ship.

A large crack and shake rocked the ship.

"Gabe, we are reaching maximum drag. Ship's integrity in jeopardy. You must quit the engine reverse." There was urgency in Feti's voice modulation.

"Got it," I replied. "Stoller, I need to let the highway take us. Can the line withstand it?"

"Better question is if they can withstand it. They're twenty yards away. Can't you give us more time?" he asked.

Another crack and shudder hit the bridge. Sparks flew from consoles.

"That seems to be a negative," I said. "Stopping reverse motion. Alex and Honora, hang on."

"Faster, Stoller," yelled Alex.

"Trying, kid. Feti, can you help me out?" asked Stoller.

"Affirmative," said Feti calmly.

"Whoa," both kids yelled as Feti accelerated the pull-in process of the external line they were latched to.

"You're going to give them whiplash, Feti," said Stoller.

"Sorry. But the speed is necessary," it replied.

"Ten yards, five yards," Stoller counted down. "Slow it down, Feti."

We heard a "Hmmph" from the kids as we watched from a back ship camera a suited up Stoller catching them at the hatch door.

My chest pains stopped as soon as I saw the kids inside.

"Close that door, Stoller," I said.

"Copy that," he said, obliging.

"Welcome back, Honora," said Zara.

Talia ran off the bridge to greet her sister.

"I think I'll be part of the welcoming committee, too," said Synthia as she shuffled off, following Talia.

I sank into my seat and put the *Alyssia* back to her normal speed. The cracking hull sounds ceased. "How's the damage, Feti?"

"Repairable, Gabe. But we will need some assistance for it," replied Feti.

"Copy that," I said. "Stoller, can you come to the bridge?"

"I'll be right up," he said.

"Goggins, keep tracking Honora's ship," I said.

"Will do. I guess we can stop calling it Honora's ship now," Goggins replied as he worked on his navigation console. "It's the Mawzian cyborgs' ship now."

I watched the ship full of cybs trail us.

"Feti, get our weapons system up and ready to launch," I said.

"Affirmative," it said.

Stoller came running. He looked out the starboard window. "Are those Mawzians actually piloting the ship?" he asked. "Aren't they blind?"

"Yes, most likely. And since Stefano activated their code, they probably are able to see —vibrationally," I said.

"And they have Gabe's pilot programs. And they're more than Mawzian miners. They're cyborgs. A military platoon as capable as Gabe and as gifted as the Kell children," said Zara.

Stoller slumped into the co-commander seat. He turned around to Stefano, who had quieted down and was also straining to look out the starboard window. A small but discreet smile crossed Stefano's face. Stoller aimed his gun at him.

"Whoa, whoa!" yelled Goggins.

"Stoller, calm down," said Zara.

Stefano jerked back in his chair and covered his head with his arms.

In one move, I swung my arm over to Stoller and pulled the gun out of his hand. "Stoller!" I snapped.

He shot me a look of hate as he jumped up. "We need to fix this situation," he said in frustration.

I stood up and pushed Stoller back into his chair. "We need to address this calmly," I said. I sat down. Everyone was silent. I handed the gun back to Stoller, who put it back in his holster. "First things first. We've got a ship full of cyborgs that can exit this highway at any moment. What are we going to do about that?"

"Weapon system ready, Gabe," said Feti.

"What? You're just going to blow away a group of Mawzians?" said Stefano. "They are a part of you, Gabe."

"No, they aren't," I said, turning toward Stefano. He was trying to control the conversation.

"Stefano, tell us how to reverse the code," said Zara.

"You're such a good hacker, *Dr.* Zara, can't you figure it out?" asked Stefano.

Stoller leaped for Stefano and struck him across the face. "Gabe may not let me shoot you, but I can beat the crap out of you. Now tell us — is this reversible?"

Stefano turned his face back to Stoller. "No, it's not."

"We need to engage with the Mawzian ship and terminate them," I said.

Honora entered the bridge followed by Talia, Synthia and Alex. "That's murder," said Honora.

"Those cybs are programmed to kill and can self-heal. They could kill hundreds or thousands unless we stop them now," I explained. My frustration level was peaking. I tried to lower my synthetic neuron levels.

"I don't believe a word that Stefano says. Honora and I could try to hack their code. We haven't even tried," said Zara.

"Honora, how many cybs are on that ship?" I asked.

"Twenty," she said.

"They're exiting. They're leaving the highway," yelled Goggins as he stared at his screens. We looked out and saw the Mawzian ship turn off the exit.

"I'm following them," I said. "We need to at least disable their ship."

"Okay," said Honora. "Disable it."

We both exited the highway, and the Mawzian ship accelerated. I pushed our engines into high gear. In a few seconds, our acceleration came to a halt.

"Feti, what's the problem?" I asked.

"Those repairs we needed, Gabe? They're affecting our engine speed. Sorry," said Feti.

I slammed my hands on the console. We lost our chance. I

moved my hands down to my lap. I didn't like showing emotion, especially frustration, in front of the team.

We watched the Mawzian ship speed farther and farther into deep space.

"There they go," said Goggins.

Stefano began laughing. He finally quieted down and then all we could hear was the distant pounding of Anjori as she slammed the doors of the airlock chamber.

Twenty cybs were hurling across the galaxy with direct orders to kill enemies of the Heragi Empire, and all we could do was watch them get farther away from us in space.

12

I reviewed the damage we sustained in the engineering room with Honora since she had the same spaceship technical specs and repair programs the Kells had programmed in my CPU. It was good to get away from everyone. The bridge was getting too crowded for my taste.

I bent down and pulled up two floor grates to get a better look at the engine fiber connectors that Feti had pointed me toward checking.

Honora had changed out of her environmental suit and cleaned up. Zara had wanted her to be checked out for any injuries, but Honora brushed her off since she could self-heal any wounds she had sustained from the cybs.

Honora sat on the floor. She passed me tools as I asked for them. She was quiet. I scanned her bio-metrics. Although her levels were hovering around normal, something wasn't right. She hadn't discussed the fighting that took place in order for her to leap out of the Mawzian ship. She must have hurt a few of them, and I didn't think she could self-heal memories of that and what she saw.

"You know I could have done what you told me to do," said Honora.

"Terminate the cybs? I know you could have," I said as I worked on the engine.

"What if I made the wrong call by letting them live?" she asked.

"You do your best to correct it," I said.

Silence.

"And you hope those who are impacted forgive you," I said, thinking of her mother Ava.

"Yeah," she said. "I think I made the right call."

"That is fine, too," I told her. And it was. Even if it wouldn't have been my call.

I finished as much of the repairs as I was capable of on the engines. I would have to report back to Stoller and the team that we needed experts to finish the job.

I placed the grates back on the floor and offered my hand to Honora for her to stand. She hugged me. She leaned back, and I could see her eyes. They were blue like her mother's. Even with my code and her gifts, I must remember that she was only fifteen years old, and her exterior bravado was a mask at times.

"Your mother and father would be very proud of you, Honora," I said.

She nodded and wiped away a tear.

"Maybe not the stealing a ship part," I said. "I may be a bad influence on you for that."

"Or your code is," she said. She let out a small laugh.

It was good to see her smile. My chest warmed.

"Let's get back and talk with the team. We don't have the tools for the final repairs that are needed."

We met the team in the galley after Stoller locked Stefano back in a staff quarters room.

Everyone grabbed a meal that Feti had prepared for them.

Anjori's pounding had stopped, which was more unnerving than when she was trying to breach the airlock doors.

"The *Alyssia* needs advanced repairs. We lack the tools for that. We need a real repair station," I explained. "How far is Oliveria?"

"It's closer than Charbeaux Station," replied Stoller. "We're just a few exits away and half a sol after that."

"The Oliverians will help us, right?" asked Goggins. "I mean, we did rescue one of their generals. Even though she is a crazy cyborg trying to kill us."

"I can't imagine they'll be happy about that part," Stoller said as he drank his gin with no meal. I wished he would eat his food rather than drink it. But that was Stoller.

"You did risk your life, and ours, to rescue her," said Zara. "I still think there has to be a coding solution."

"There better be, or we just unleashed the end of any Heragi rebel resistance on the galaxy," said Goggins around a bite.

"Charbeaux Station is the closest transfer point, correct, Stoller?" I asked.

"Yes, they would be headed there I would guess," he said.

"Then that's where we need to go," said Alex.

"No, we need to return Anjori," said Stoller.

"And retrieve your spaceship?" asked Alex. "Does that have something to do with it?"

"You're blasted right it does," snapped Stoller. "My ship is fast. And as I said before, two ships are better than one, right, kid?"

"We need to warn someone at Charbeaux Station," I said. They can detain the ship. "Stoller, is there someone you trust who can help?"

"Trust? That cuts down the number. Most of them, even though they are apolitical, are not fans of the Heragi Empire.

Some may ask why get involved if the cybs aren't targeting them. I'm not sure how we can get *any* of them involved."

"These cybs have code that is mutating. Changing every hour," said Synthia, who stood up and looked out of the galley window into deep space. "They may not be the enemy now, but that could change at any moment, on the Empire's whim to change the scope of what defines an enemy. Travelers, tradesmen, aliens, green eyes, yellow skin — they could become the Empire's enemy too."

Her words weighed heavily on everyone.

"I should have killed them all while I had the chance," Honora said.

Talia shook her head and raised her arm comm. "We will contact Uncle Jeb. He will help us."

"Yes, Uncle Jebediah," said Alex.

Stoller nodded. "Good. And I do have a friend who's a manager at the Charbeaux Station's planet-port. They can help with a message relay."

I got up to leave. "Stoller, are you done with your meal?"

He slammed his shot of gin. "Just finished." He headed back to the bridge with Goggins.

As I followed after them, Synthia grabbed my hand and pulled me back.

"There's something more you need to know about the cyborgs," she said to me and Zara.

"Tell us," I said.

"They're not just going out on a search and destroy mission," she whispered. "They're going out to assimilate all of the Heragi and rebel planets. To be imbedded in their societies. To marry, to breed, to be entrenched in their communities — at all levels. You will never know who is a cyborg and who is not in the rebel communities."

Zara stepped forward. "Unless we test. We can find differentiators."

"We do have a test subject," I said.

"Anjori," said Zara.

"Yes," I answered.

"Her family will never allow it," said Zara.

"If they want her back to the way she was, they will," said Synthia.

"Stoller won't like it," said Alex.

"Stoller doesn't like anything but his ship and his gin," said Zara.

"And you," said Synthia.

Zara looked up, surprised by Synthia's comment.

"You may have to reason with him later, Zara," I said, turning to leave the galley.

Back on the bridge, Stoller was working with Feti on a comms relay to the Charbeaux Station. He began recording his message that would be sent off. I took my seat and steered us back onto the Karakova Highway.

"Leroy, this is Stoller. Buddy, I need a favor. There's a trade ship coming off the K Highway. It's Mawzian. Orange with black thrusters. ID is BZ42-854, but they will probably scrub that identification number by the time they reach you. Delay them as long as you can. They're pretty dangerous. Do a body count when they arrive and leave. There should be twenty of them. I'll keep in touch."

Stoller was about to send the message when he had a second thought.

"One more thing — they're bad. Real bad. Put out word to everyone on the docks that they should be on alert. Oh, and I'll knock off three thousand credits from the quinker total you owe me. Stay safe. Stoller out."

He ended the message. It was a tough message to send. He

swung his seat around to the Kell children, who had arrived on the bridge. "Where the blasters is your uncle?"

Geez. Stoller. I'd need to give him a sensitivity talk later. I was sure he'd love that, especially coming from a robot.

"Easy," said Goggins. Even he had some civility training.

"Sorry, kids. Where do you believe your Uncle Jebediah is located at this present time?" He looked at Goggins and rolled his eyes to basically say, *how's that?*

The children huddled and talked amongst themselves in the sign language their parents had created just for them. I knew it too, so I could pick up on the conversation. Alex nodded, and they all went back to their seats.

"Really?" asked Stoller. "Did we need a union meeting for an answer?" He laughed. No one else did.

"We left before he had finalized his plans," said Alex.

"We'll have to contact our parents on Zaradorba," said Honora. "They can help us."

I swung around to look out in space. *Great.*

Talia read my thought and sent one back to me. *It's the only way.*

Reminder to myself — I'd need to watch my thoughts around the children and Synthia. I turned back around in my seat. "Zara, can you work on a comm message to Ava and Damiel? Feti and Goggins can find a nearby satellite to utilize," I said.

"Copy that," said Zara as she turned to Goggins to begin a comms transmission.

Stoller turned back to the front bridge window. He looked out at the stars and planets. He pulled up his fingers and displayed various configurations with them. He pulled them down and nodded.

"There. Take the next exit," he said.

"Copy that," I said, turning the *Alyssia* toward the exit.

"See that yellow planet with the four rings?" He pointed. "That's Oliveria."

"It's beautiful," said Talia's transceiver.

"Sure is," said Stoller. "I spent a lot of time on that planet. Good times and a few bad ones, too." A melancholy mood had hit Stoller. Or perhaps it was fear.

"They won't be too hard on you. You're bringing back their leader's sister," said Zara as she put her hand on his shoulder.

"Ten years is a long time." He got up, letting her hand slide off his shoulder. "I'm going to check on Anjori." He left the bridge.

Zara watched him leave and went back to working with Alex on the message to send to Ava and Damiel. I hoped Ava knew I didn't want her children to run away and join us. What did it matter anymore? She could think what she wanted to think.

I put the ship on auto-pilot with Feti in charge of the navigation to Oliveria. I got up and headed to the airlock chamber to check on Stoller.

When I arrived at the chamber, Stoller had a water bottle and some protobars in his hands. He was looking through the airlock window, trying to reason with Anjori. "I've got food and water for you," he said through the wall intercom.

I peered into the second airlock window to view Anjori. She was sitting on the floor with her back against the exterior door, staring up at us.

She didn't answer him.

"What are you doing? We can't open this door," I said.

"She hasn't eaten or drank anything since we don't know when. I don't want to deliver a corpse to her sister, Swina."

"She'll be fine," I said. "We don't know how Stefano's coding might have affected the cybs' bio systems. They may be able to go days without food or water."

Then Anjori put up her hands and reached up to Stoller. She touched her throat and nodded. She was trying to tell him she was thirsty.

"She's human, Gabe," he said, watching her.

"She's a killer cyborg," I said.

He put his head down and shook it. He dropped the bottle and bars. "Blasted. I should have tried to rescue her sooner."

Yes, he should have.

Anjori was now staring at me. I turned and headed back to the bridge.

Don't trust him. The thought was pushed into my head. It wasn't my thought. I turned around, expecting one of the Kell children. No one was behind me.

He's weak. Another thought came into my mind.

Anjori was using her telepathic coding. I closed my visor view and went into my mind to build the cube that Synthia had taught me to utilize telepathic messaging — and for protection. Anjori appeared inside my cube as if she were waiting for me. She started to circle me, like a predator.

Your code is in me, she thought.

So I hear, I thought back.

Then you're my sibling. Like a brother.

I wouldn't say that. In fact, don't say that. You're a knock off. A bad one, at that.

I have a mission just like you do.

Your mission is false. It's corrupted. Delete it.

Why would I do that?

To get back to what you were. What you are. You're Anjori Oliveria. A great general. Sister to Swina Oliveria, the leader of your providence.

My sister, who let me rot in that prison for ten years?

I heard the sound of the airlock chamber door beginning to open. I pushed down the walls of my cube and focused my eyesight back to the chamber door. Stoller was opening it.

"No! Stop," I yelled, lunging for the door.

Anjori had jumped toward the door and was already prying it open with her fingers. Stoller, as if waking from a daze, quickly realized his error and helped me push back on the doors. Anjori began a high-pitched scream that was aimed to disorient us. Stoller grabbed his head in pain. I pushed with all my strength and managed to shut the door. It locked.

I fell against the adjacent wall. "What were you thinking?"

"I don't know. I was walking after you when I heard a voice, her voice, in my head. She said she was thirsty. She said she wouldn't try to get out," he explained as he got up from his knees.

"She was using her telepathic powers," I said. "Get out of here."

Stoller looked back one more time at Anjori, who was now pacing in the airlock, and then he left for the bridge.

I sent Anjori a thought. *Can the other Mawzian cyborgs do what you just did?*

Yes. Can't you?

I can't implant thoughts into those who aren't already telepathic.

That's too bad. I seem to be version 2.0 of you. You need an upgrade. I'm sure Stefano will help you with that.

No thanks.

Then, I'm more rogue than you? She smirked.

We'll get you back, Anjori. To what you used to be.

Who said I want that? I was a prisoner for ten years. If I had these powers, I could have broken out years ago. I like who I am.

That's just crap code that Stefano has brainwashed you with talking. We're going to fix that.

What? Don't you dare. Don't touch me. I won't let you or anyone near me.

We'll see about that, or else.

Or else what?

Or else I'll be the one to end you.

Anjori grunted. *I'm stronger than you in every way.*

You may be, but I have a mission, too.

Yes, I know it. Stefano had a big laugh in the lab when he read the code. Save the children, right?

Right.

Noble. But who will save you? Your own creators planned on killing you. That must be so painful for you — the feeling robot.

Where did you learn that?

From you. I've been poking around in your mind since the medbay.

We're done here.

Anjori stared at me as code flashed over her pupils.

I turned and walked away.

13

———————

Back on the bridge, Zara and the children worked on an encrypted message to send to Ava and Damiel. Zara asked Goggins to finish sending the message, and she pulled me to the side.

"What's wrong with Stoller?" she asked.

"He's too close to Anjori. It's affecting his decision making. She can break into minds," I said. "We'll have to keep him away from her."

"Copy that," said Zara.

I sat down in the commander seat and looked over to Stoller. He was slumped in the co-commander seat. He stared off into space, rubbing his chin. His guilt was tearing him up, I was sure, but I needed him to hold it together as a senior member of this team.

Emotions are contagious, and I didn't need the crew on the *Alyssia* to doubt or feel guilt or re-think past decisions that Stoller could spread to them. In fact, that was good for me to remember as well.

"Gabe, we've sent the message to Ava and Damiel," said Goggins.

"They should know where Uncle Jeb is headed," said Alex.

"Good. Time to contact the Oliverian leadership. We've just entered into their providence," I said. He didn't respond. "Stoller," I said louder.

He pulled out of his daydream in a startle. "What?" He was disorientated.

"We need to contact Anjori's sister and tell her we'll be landing soon." I leaned into Stoller and whispered, "I need you to hold it together. Do you copy?" I put my hand on his shoulder.

He looked down at my hand. He pulled away. He bucked up. "Yeah, I'm fine. Okay, let's do it."

"Feti, Stoller is going to give you directions to follow as we approach the Oliveria Providence."

"Affirmative, Gabe," said Feti. "Please proceed, Stoller."

"Feti, orient the ship to the Oliverian city of Yusses. They have a planet-port. Get ahold of their traffic tower. Ask for permission to land. Try to get us comms with their senior official there. Tell them we are requesting an audience with Swina Oliveria. They can put us in touch with one of Swina's commanders."

"Copy that, Stoller," said Feti.

An alert flashed on my monitor.

"Gabe, two ships. Starboard and port side," reported Feti.

"Got 'em," I said. "They've got target locks on us."

"Heading to the guns," said Alex as he got up.

"No," Stoller said. "These are Oliverian ships."

"Stoller is correct. Their hull IDs scan as Oliverian Naval," said Feti.

Alex sat back down. "And the target-lock?"

"Just protecting themselves, Alex. They've learned over the centuries. You got to know who's in your skies or space," retorted Stoller. I could tell he was pulling out of his dark mood. Good. I needed him back.

"I have a comm link to the Yusses planet-port," Feti reported.

"Go ahead, Stoller," I said.

Stoller leaned in on his seat and propped himself up. "Give me both video and audio, Feti." He cleared his throat and straightened his hair and then his shirt. It was funny to see him worried about his appearance.

On the comm screen, a hologram of a man in military fatigues appeared. The man was large, with a similar body type as Anjori, expansive shoulders outlined in his uniform.

"This is James Stoller, former captain of the Degasian Marines."

"Captain?" whispered Zara.

"James?" whispered back Alex.

"Marines?" said Honora loudly.

Stoller turned and gave Honora a harsh look. "Yeah, marines, kid." He turned back to the monitor camera. "Who am I speaking with?"

The man on the camera hardened his brow. "Stoller? You've got nerve showing up in our providence unannounced."

Stoller swore under his breath. "Air Commander Vauser. It's been a while."

"To what do we owe the pleasure?" Vauser growled. "And tell me why I should grant you landing rights?"

"I'll cut to the chase. I've got Anjori," said Stoller. "We rescued her off Mawzi."

Vauser's facial expression changed to surprise. "Granting permission to land."

The comm link ended.

Stoller let out a sigh of relief.

"Feti, prepare us for landing," I said and flicked on the comms to Stefano's quarters. "Stefano, buckle up, we're landing." I didn't bother notifying Anjori. She could see we were landing through the airlock window and hang on to a wall grip. If she got knocked out for a while, that could only help us.

The Oliverian navy ships escorted us down and then peeled off when we entered the planet's atmosphere. The Oliverian planet was green and plush. We flew over large bodies of water and expansive plains before we came upon the golden city of Yusses.

Everyone peered out of the bridge windows and were silent as the beautiful city with rivers, bridges and rounded buildings was laid out before us.

"It's gorgeous," said Talia's transceiver.

"It sure is, kid. I once thought I would live out the rest of my years here," said Stoller in a soft tone that I'd never heard from him.

"What do they trade? How do they make money?" asked Zara.

"They're self-sustaining. They have every resource a civilization needs, and they never ran into an over-population problem. But when they do need some inter-planetary trade, they have large reserves of gold. That is why other planets attack them. And why they aren't the most trusting of people," explained Stoller.

We flew toward the planet-port and were directed to land at a gate close to tower control.

We touched ground, and I shut down the engines. Honora helped Talia unbuckle from her seat constraints, and Alex was already out of his seat.

Synthia looked like she was meditating, which was fine. We needed all the serenity we could muster.

"Feti, keep the ship on lockdown. We still have Anjori secured in the airlock," I said.

"Affirmative, Gabe," it said.

"What's the plan?" asked Goggins as he unbuckled from his seat.

"Stoller?" I asked.

"Return Anjori to her family," said Stoller with a shrug.

"In the state she's in?" asked Zara.

"First off, how do we expect to move Anjori out of the airlock?" asked Goggins. "Thank goodness she stopped pounding; it was giving me a bloody headache."

"We're going to reduce the oxygen and increase the CO2. When she passes out, we will then secure her for a move to an Oliverian location," I said.

Stoller straightened up. "That could kill her."

"There's a risk, but I doubt it," I said.

"I'm glad you *doubt* it. But I *doubt* that Anjori's sister would agree with or support this strategy," he said as he unbuckled from his seat.

I rose and pointed to Alex to follow me. "That's why we should do it as soon as possible. Honora and Zara, I need you."

"Stoller, send a comm to have a secure transport available for Anjori when we open the airlock," I said. "And you better tell them what state of mind Anjori is in."

Stoller swore. I ignored him and marched down the hallway to the airlock.

"Zara, grab as many tranquilizer shots as you can find in the medbay," I said as we neared the center of the ship. Zara peeled off.

"Suit up. We're going to have Feti stop the air flow into the chamber," I explained as we arrived at the equipment room.

Honora and Alex grabbed spacesuits and began pulling them on. Zara ran into the room with a handful of tranquilizer shots. She passed them out to each of us and got her suit on.

I looked into the equipment room and saw that the *Alyssia* had a stretcher with wheels. Perfect. I pulled it out and prepped it next to the airlock door.

"Feti?"

"Yes, Gabe?"

"On my order, in the air chamber, stop the oxygen flow and increase CO2. No one is allowed to override my order. Understand?" I instructed.

"Affirmative, Gabe. But —" it started

"No buts," I said firmly.

"Copy that," it said.

I turned to the others. "All set?"

They nodded and gave affirmative replies. I opened a comm link to all their suits.

"When Anjori falters, then I will scan her bio-levels. Only then will we go in and secure her to the gurney," I explained. "Another thing. She has the power of telepathy. She can get into your head. You need to not let her in. Do you understand?"

Zara and Honora gave me affirmative responses.

"And the tranquilizers?" Alex asked.

"Administer them on my command. Once she begins to awaken," I said.

They nodded and gave a thumbs up.

I opened up a comm to the bridge. "Stoller, is there a transport ready to take her?"

"Affirmative, I see them rolling up now," said Stoller. "I'm coming down."

"No, stay there," I ordered.

Silence.

He was already on his way. I didn't want him to witness this — it wouldn't be pretty.

Goggins got on the comm. "He's headed back to you."

"Yeah, I figured. Keep Synthia and Talia up near you," I replied.

"Copy that," said Goggins. "I prefer it here."

I peered into the airlock chamber window. Anjori stood calmly looking out the window. She was near her home planet.

Gone for ten years. By this time, she could see a team of Oliverian military assembling outside the ship, not to welcome her with cheers but to subdue her.

"Okay, Feti, go ahead. Slowly," I ordered.

Stoller arrived and glanced through the airlock window. His face showed no emotion. I did a bio-level scan on him and indeed his levels were calm. I was glad to see that.

In a few minutes, I could see Anjori's legs falter. She turned and looked all around the room. She began to understand what was happening. She looked at me through the window. She fell to her knees.

I couldn't do a bio-metrics scan of Anjori through the metal, so I had to rely on the wall monitor bio-scans. I pushed a few buttons and read her levels. Her system was strong. She tried to control her breathing and meditate.

Honora and Alex groaned and grabbed their heads. She was trying to break into their minds.

I opened a comm back up to the bridge. "Goggins, we need Synthia. Send her down, fast."

"Copy that. She's on her way," said Goggins.

"What's happening? Is Anjori trying to kill them?" asked Stoller as he kneeled to help Honora and Alex.

"I don't know," I replied. And I didn't.

"Stop her. Turn her oxygen back on. Scrub the CO2," he yelled.

"No," I said. "We just need a few more minutes."

"Feti, turn the oxygen back on," yelled Stoller.

"I'm sorry, Stoller. I can't do that," said Feti.

Honora and Alex writhed in pain on the ground.

Stoller jumped up. "How can you watch them? You're supposed to protect them, or did you forget your prime directive?" He pushed against my chest.

I looked through the airlock window. Anjori was still on her knees.

My chest started hurting. It pained me to watch the children suffer, but all my risk calculations told me to have Feti continue the process.

Synthia ran up and saw the children. She was about to kneel when I grabbed her arm. "Save them by stopping her." I guided her to the airlock window.

She looked back at the children and then into the airlock. She closed her eyes, and I knew she was building her mind sphere that I had once visited when she first trained me and Talia to communicate with each other in our minds.

Talia and Goggins ran toward us. Talia looked at Synthia and stopped — she also closed her eyes and went into her mind.

We needed all the help we could get.

I quieted my systems and went into my mind. I saw Synthia's mind sphere and walked into it with Talia.

Stand down, thought Synthia to Anjori.

That goes against my prime directive, thought Anjori.

You're being used.

My prime directive must be obeyed.

Synthia raised her hands. *You will not harm these children.*

Honora and Alex stopped writhing.

Anjori started to fade from Synthia's sphere.

We all opened our eyes. Anjori was lying face down in the airlock.

"Gabe, Anjori is unconscious," said Feti.

"Thank you, Feti. Stop adding the CO2." I turned to Synthia and Talia. "You need to leave the area. Goggins, take them." I glanced at Stoller. "You too. Go."

Goggins guided Synthia and Talia back up the hallway, followed by Stoller.

Zara helped Alex and Honora to their feet.

"Feti, open the door!" I yelled.

I readied the gurney as Feti opened the door.

We ran in and heaved the warrior onto the bed. I slammed

open the airlock door leading out to the ramp. There was an Oliverian medical team waiting for her. We were strapping her down when she began to wake.

"Zara, your tranquilizer," I said.

Zara grabbed the shot and stabbed it into Anjori's bicep.

The medical team stepped in. A lead medic pushed me aside. "We'll take it from here."

"She's strong," I warned as they took her down the ramp.

"All our warriors are," the medic replied.

We were left standing on the ramp looking at one another. Zara hugged the children and Stoller came down.

"That was one heck of a welcome home for a hero," said Stoller as he stared at me.

"Did you have a better idea?" I asked, stepping up to him chest to chest.

"Boys, boys. Not in front of the children," said Zara as she separated us.

I felt footsteps on the ramp and turned to see who was approaching. A woman dressed in a combat suit hiked up. She was eight feet tall and built like Anjori. They did build big people on this planet.

The Oliverian woman was followed by six soldiers armed with guns.

"Captain Stoller. Nice to see you again," she said.

Stoller stepped around me and extended his hand to the woman. "Captain Bre, is that true?"

"Since you have one of our soldiers, then yes. Otherwise, if I had never seen your face again that would have been fine by me. And I'm Admiral Bre now," she said.

"Congratulations," said Stoller.

"I don't relish it. Swina Oliverian gave me the promotion when her sister became imprisoned, no thanks to you," she spit out.

"At least I went back and got her," said Stoller.

Admiral Bre and Stoller stared each other down. I left the two seething colleagues on the ramp and marched back into the *Alyssia* to assemble everyone so we could continue on to the necessary meetings with the Oliverians.

This was going to be a fun visit.

14

Oliverian guards shuttled us from the *Alyssia* to their planet intelligence agency building in downtown Yusses. The building was impressive as all the buildings were in their capital city. It was architecturally pleasing, with gold-covered fountains and an expansive atrium in the entryway.

On the second floor, they guided us into a large computer room where they already had Anjori induced in a coma lying on a table with monitors scanning all of her vitals. The room was circular and bright. The ceilings were tall, obviously suited for the large frames of Oliverians. Various medical technicians shuffled from monitor to monitor and conferred with each other.

I was just happy they had kept Anjori unconscious.

Stoller circled the perimeter of the room like a caged animal. He glanced alternately at Anjori lying motionless on the table and out the windows of the room. His uncomfortableness was making me uncomfortable. I didn't bother to scan his biometrics. I knew they were high.

The children were quiet like they were in a sacred space. Perhaps they were. Alex took a seat and watched everyone. Probably doing a reconnaissance as he was trained at the Academy. Memorizing door entrances and exits, the people in the room and their comings and goings.

Honora and Zara reviewed the computers and medical equipment, knowing that code discussions would begin quickly.

Talia guided Synthia to a chair as a granddaughter would guide a grandmother. Since leaving Mawzi, Synthia hadn't had much time to rest and recuperate. Heck, since we rescued her from Suissey on our last mission, she hadn't had a rest, come to think of it. She moved slowly, and I made a note in my system to ask the Oliverians to give her a medical review. Of course, Synthia may not agree to that plan.

Goggins sat in a chair with his arms folded. He appeared impatient. His foot tapped. He was either hungry or craving coffee. Either way, I knew to expect some snippy comments from him as the Oliverians began questioning us.

Talia noticed me sitting by myself. She sent me a thought. *This place is amazing.*

Yes, it's a beautiful city.

I'm so glad we were able to rescue Anjori. It's a two-fer, remember? She giggled.

My heart warmed. I hadn't felt it do that for a while. I nodded. *Yes. And I'm glad, too.*

They'll be able to fix Anjori, won't they?

I had calculated a few scenarios earlier on our ride over, but really, I didn't know.

I hope so, was the best thought I could muster.

Believe.

I want to believe.

Me too.

She stopped sending me her thoughts and sat holding Synthia's hand.

Two armed soldiers entered. They swept the room with their eyes and then motioned the all-clear sign to someone out in the hallway.

An Oliverian woman entered, regal and holding her head high. I knew before it was announced that this was Swina Oliverian, prime minister of the Oliveria Providence.

She scanned the room like a trained military soldier. To say that she had a mystique was an understatement. She held the room. She smiled. It was a perfect smile. And then she spoke.

"I want to thank you all for returning my beloved sister, Anjori. Although she is injured, we pray and will work diligently to bring her back to us in full health and vitality. Thank you for your courage." She turned directly to Stoller who had his head turned down. "And perseverance."

A guard led Swina to a seat at the front of the room. She was flanked by a woman in a white coat and a man in a blue suit. "Please sit," Swina said.

Admiral Bre entered the room and quietly leaned against a window. She exchanged glances with Stoller.

"Captain Stoller, it's good to see you. Thank you for returning my sister," said Swina.

Stoller nodded and briefly glanced up. "Sorry it took so long."

Swina smiled with no sign of hostility and nodded.

Then a young Oliverian man entered the room. He wore sunglasses and dressed in a fly suit, the kind pilots often wore. He leaned over to Swina and kissed her on the cheek. The young man then approached Anjori and touched her hand gently. He turned and took a seat to the side.

"Stoller, you know my son, Tristan," Swina said with a motion of her hand to the young man.

Stoller nodded. "Yes, how could I forget?"

Tristan smiled widely and took off his sunglasses. "Been too long, Stoller. I'd just come in on the *Ravena* when I heard the news."

That was a conversation opener, I thought.

"The *Ravena* was Stoller's ship," said Alex as he nudged me in the chest.

"I know," I whispered. Great, two pilots getting into it over a ship. I couldn't wait for this.

"It's still in great shape," said Tristan.

"Thanks for taking care of it," said Stoller. "But I'm going to need it back now."

I almost slapped my head with my hand. Nothing like jumping right into it, Stoller.

Tristan scoffed, and his mother raised her hand to stop him from replying. "For your heroics, I'm sure we can arrange for the transfer of the *Ravena* back to you, Captain Stoller."

Tristan twisted in his seat but knew better than to go against her in public. The best he could do was roll his eyes.

"Thank you," said Stoller, and then he muttered under his breath, "He cheated, that's how he won it."

"What did you say?" asked Tristan with a hand to his ear.

"Enough, moving on," commanded Swina.

Now that Stoller got what he wanted, we could press on to more important matters. Thank goodness.

"Robot," Swina said. Her voice made me straighten in my chair, and I was already straight.

"Yes, ma'am," I said. "They call me Gabe."

"Gabe is a male name. But you are a robot. Neither male nor female, correct?"

I hadn't thought of that before, but she was correct.

"Yes, ma'am. My creators —"

"Ava and Damiel Kell? These children's parents?" interrupted the woman in white sitting next to Swina, pointing at the Kell children.

"This is Dr. Rashel, lead geneticist and researcher here at our hospital," said Swina. Dr. Rashel smiled and glanced back at me.

"Yes, Ava and Damiel Kell are my creators. And these are their children. Alex, Honora and Talia."

"Yes, we know," said the man in the blue suit. "Each with unique skills, and also we have their mentor, Synthia, most recently a Heragi prisoner."

The man got the attention of a soldier. He pointed to the door. The soldier opened the door, and they led in Stefano and sat him down.

"Kept captive by Dr. Stefano. Who also was experimenting on Anjori," said the man in the blue suit. "We are also aware that their uncle is Jebediah Kell, a Heragi rebel leader."

"Yes, that is all correct," I answered. My neuron levels were rising. I felt an urge to twist in my seat but fought it off. I rationalized that they needed to verify our backgrounds for security reasons. Fair enough. But I didn't like how it felt.

"Let me introduce my Chief of Staff, Mr. Jazar," said Swina, pointing to the man in the blue suit who nodded to us.

"And then we have crew member Dr. Goggins. Impressive educational background but also wanted by the Heragi."

"Wanted?" chirped Goggins. "For questioning only, correct?"

"No. For aiding and abetting known enemies of the Heragi Empire," said Jazar.

"Dr. Zara Lorgia, known also for her expertise in computer science, coding, hacking and —" started Jazar.

"Stop stating what you and we already know. Are we on trial?" Zara snapped.

"No, please excuse my leaders," said Swina. "We just want to make sure we understand the situation."

"The situation is that your sister is now a cyborg," Zara said. "And we need to figure out a solution to un-cyborg her." Zara leaned back, then added, "Ma'am."

If I could roll my eyes, I would. My crew needed tutorials on interpersonal communications. Perhaps the communication code Ava uploaded to my directory could be shared at our next crew meeting. This was embarrassing.

Honora spoke up. Thank goodness we shared some of the

same communication files. "Pardon me, but we have a lot of work to do in a very short amount of time. I think that is what Zara is getting at." Honora looked to me.

"Right now, there is a ship of Mawzians that Dr. Stefano genetically modified with my code —" I began.

"You mean rogue code. You can kill whoever you want," Dr. Rashel interrupted.

Boy, this was getting frustrating, but they did have to know what they were dealing with.

"Yes, that is correct. But those Mawzians also have the children's DNA, as does Anjori. This combination is very dangerous. They must be stopped — or altered," I added. I hoped they weren't offended by my *stopped* wording which could easily be replaced by the word terminated.

Silence for a moment.

"Dangerous to *who*?" Swina asked.

"Stefano programmed them with a prime directive to kill all enemies of the Heragi Empire," said Zara. "Your sister tried to take out everyone on our ship."

Swina nodded but didn't say anything. Jazar leaned over and whispered into Swina's ear. Swina nodded. "I'm sorry that happened. Our medical team would love to collaborate with you and your team on a solution. We want to cure my sister and help everyone afflicted by Dr. Stefano," she said. "That is why we brought him here. We will begin immediately."

"And what do you think will make me help you?" said Stefano with his head cocked to the side.

"We are soon to receive a Heragi guest," said Tristan, who typed on his arm comm, and a hologram appeared in the center of the room. The hologram screen showed General Foxwell's ship landing at Yusses' planet-port.

"That's Foxwell's ship," I said.

"Yes," said Tristan. "He's your boss, isn't he, Stefano?"

Stefano nodded.

"I don't have to tell you to cooperate, but he will," said Tristan.

"Don't be too sure of that," said Stefano.

"What is a Heragi general doing visiting the Oliveria Providence?" asked Zara. "Are you collaborating with them?"

"They are courting us. And as any woman knows, there is a difference between being courted and showing up with a ring and a wedding date," said Swina with a grin.

"They want to form an alliance. We accepted the meeting on our planet as a courtesy. We do not want to upset them until we know what they want. We had no idea they were on Mawzi," said Jazar.

"We're wasting time here," said Stoller as he rose from his seat. "I have friends on Charbeaux Station who are in real danger. There is a ship full of cyborg Mawzians about to show up there, and I don't want any more people hurt."

"I'm coming with you," said Alex as he jumped up.

"Great. Follow me." Stoller began to walk out of the room.

What?

Talia ran over to her brother and wrapped her arms around his waist. *Stop him,* she yelled into my mind.

"No." I stood up and grabbed Alex's shoulder.

I felt like we were having a family squabble in front of strangers — and I guess we were.

"Gabe," said Honora as she got between Alex and me. She touched my arm and I released his shoulder. Honora turned to her brother. "Mom and Dad would want us to stay together," she said.

"Did you think about that when you stole the ship from Mawzi?" he said in a gentle tone.

"No. I wanted to help them," she said.

"As do I," he said. Alex kissed Honora on the forehead and hugged Talia. "I'll stay in touch and send messages to the *Alyssia.*"

"I could use a good wing-man," said Stoller, looking at me. "I'll watch over him. Promise."

Zara said, "Thanks for sticking around."

"You had your chance. You snooze, you lose," Stoller said with a laugh. If she could walk up to Stoller and smack him, I was sure she would, but she moved forward, thought twice, and then leaned back in her seat and just shook her head.

"Hmmph, pilots," she muttered under her breath.

Stoller snapped his fingers like he forgot something. "Dad, I need to borrow the ship keys tonight."

Tristan shook his head at Stoller's joke. "Gate 891 at the planet-port. You'll have full clearance for launch."

"Thanks," said Stoller with a huge grin, and then he left with Alex.

My chest hurt.

Ava was going to hate me even more. I should just keep a checklist of all the bad things I was letting her children get involved with since she put me in charge of their safety. Even I would fire myself.

Synthia approached Anjori. "It's time we begin working on her. Her code may be mutating and becoming stronger, along with her powers. Talia and I can enter her mind when she becomes conscious. Zara, Goggins and Honora can lead with the coding."

Swina rose and stepped over to her sister and Synthia, taking her hand. "I agree. Time to get to work. Thank you, Synthia."

"And what will the robot do?" asked Tristan, pointing at me. I didn't think I liked this young man either. But he had a good point. I didn't have anything to do in this room except protect them all from being killed if Anjori broke loose.

"It's his code that runs through her DNA now, as well as my sister's. He knows his programs the best, and he will know what she is planning to do at almost the exact time she will. He's key, don't you see? It's his rogue code," said Honora.

Tristan nodded and smiled. "Then it's nice to meet you, Gabe." He reached out his hand. He was one of only a handful of humans or aliens that had done that. It made me feel as an equal, even if he needed some cajoling from Honora. We shook hands. My chest warmed.

"I'll leave you experts to all of this." Tristan bowed and left the room. Hard not to like Tristan once he warmed up. I felt somehow that he and Stoller may not be so dissimilar. Cut from the same cloth, as they say. It felt good to say that colloquialism. It'd been a while. I must remember how wonderful it felt to access them in my syntax. I was glad Ava programmed them in me.

"And definitely, you have no need for politicians," said Swina as she smiled and exited the room with Jazar and her guards.

Dr. Rashel went to Anjori's monitors and took a look. "Our staff has been reviewing her DNA samples. We should have the results soon. Tell me more about the children's DNA and gifts. Then we can move on to reviewing Gabe's code," said Dr. Rashel.

"Sounds good," said Zara. "There will be plenty of data that Honora and I can help parse through."

I stepped forward. "Does Swina understand that we'll be experimenting on her sister? It could be dangerous. It may kill her," I explained.

Dr. Rashel turned away from the monitors to face all of us. "Yes, we discussed that."

"And?" asked Synthia.

"We decided that we aren't going to experiment on Anjori," said Dr. Rashel.

"What?" I said.

"We'll be experimenting on Dr. Stefano."

Stefano jumped up in protest, and a guard pushed him back

into his chair. Two med techs injected him with a sedative. He began to lose consciousness.

"How could you? You're monsters," he said before he faded out.

"We'll code Stefano in the same way. Give him the directive to kill any Heragi enemies — and then we will begin experimenting," said Dr. Rashel.

I was a bit stunned. I didn't know what to say.

My team looked at each other. They were confused. Was this right? Were we now becoming the monsters, or were we saving the galaxy?

Maybe you have to become one to do the other. But it didn't feel right.

We all watched as they put Stefano's body on a table side-by-side with Anjori and began their procedures.

15

Goggins hooked me up to his computer in the med lab and reviewed my file directories. "So, that is how the Kells triggered your prime directive. Just with a simple voice recognition program and password," he said.

"But look, the coding was clever. It was stealth. Built behind his CPU unit code. It was encrypted not once but twice," said Zara, pointing to his screen.

"That's why I never noticed it while I worked on the navigation program. Your parents are very smart people," he said to Honora.

"Yes, they are," she replied while reviewing her siblings' and her own DNA code. "They kept our DNA gifts a secret from the Heragi government for many years."

"Are we done?" I asked Goggins. I didn't like being connected to the Oliverians' network. Or anyone's network.

"Yes, sorry, Gabe." Goggins unhooked me.

"If you need me, contact my comm. I want to take Talia outside," I said to Zara and Honora.

"Copy that," said Zara.

Honora said, "Thanks, good idea."

I sent Talia a thought. *How about we stretch our legs?*

She nodded, and I took her hand and led her out of the laboratory room that held Anjori and now Stefano on operating tables. Nearby was a bench overlooking the building's atrium. Oliverian trees and exotic plants blossomed before us. It was a beautiful setting. It was upsetting to me that Talia would be involved in or even witness the experimentation on Stefano.

We sat and looked at the trees. Oliverian music played from below, on the first floor. It was soothing. I wished Talia could hear it.

Talia closed her eyes.

She could hear it — the vibrations. She opened her eyes, turned to me and pointed at the woman playing the string instrument creating the harmonic sounds. I nodded and sent her a thought. *Can you hear the music?*

Yes, I put the musician in my mind. It's beautiful.

Yes, it is.

What's wrong?

I don't want you in the lab room. You shouldn't be watching that.

I may be able to help.

They'll contact us if they need anything.

Talia stood up and leaned over the railing to peer down at the first floor, then toward the ceiling that reached up forty more floors. *They don't have birds inside.*

Let's go walk outside then.

Talia smiled and took my hand. We took an escalator down to the entrance and left the building. We came upon a nearby park and strolled around a large concrete pond filled with ducks and Oliverians on hoverboats that slowly crossed the water. A couple passed by us, holding their child's hands on each side.

I wondered if Talia missed her parents. She probably just read that thought and this next one. I tried to stop thinking.

Talia giggled. *I do miss them. Sometimes. Is that awful of me?*

Not at all. But we can send you back to them.

No. She kneeled by the pond. She put her hand in the water and made ripples. *This is a beautiful city on a beautiful planet. I wish Heragi was like this.*

Maybe one day it can be.

Talia looked up from the pond. The sun shone on her face. She closed her eyes and squinted. Her face went expressionless. *I see war on the planet and other planets. I see Alex leading soldiers into battle. Honora is in a gold dress looking over an ocean. And I see you. You're...you're crying.* Talia opened her eyes.

Robots don't cry, I thought back to her.

I know.

You can see the future, like Synthia?

Yes, but she doesn't call it the future. She calls it thought fields. They flow, they go. We join them or not.

An Oliverian child ran by us.

Do you dream? she asked.

No...at least not yet.

We sat in silence and watch the Oliverians enjoy their park, their lives. I liked it here. I looked around, but there weren't any robots. None of any kind. But none of the Oliverians looked at me in wonder or surprise or fear. Perhaps they couldn't see me. It made me feel distant but not bad. In fact, it felt good to disappear into the landscape and forget I was a robot — on the outside.

They need us now, Talia thought.

Copy that.

My arm comm sounded, and I opened up the channel.

"Gabe, we need you and Talia back at the lab," said Zara.

"We're on our way," I said and turned the comm off.

Talia took my hand and we headed back to the hospital. As

we entered the first-floor atrium, Talia sent me a thought. *I'm going to stay inside the lab room.*

Yes, I know. You belong there as much as I do.

We entered the lab and found Dr. Rashel's techs and our team in full collaboration. Stefano was connected to multiple computers. Honora, Zara and Goggins had set up coding stations with monitors, and Synthia was seated near Stefano where she was meditating. Dr. Rashel's techs wore surgical scrubs and were about to inject Stefano from a long vial into his spinal cord.

Talia sat with Synthia. She closed her eyes and joined the meditation.

Dr. Rashel approached me.

"The injection includes the children's DNA strands?" I asked.

"Yes, and nanobots with your code," said Dr. Rashel. "We can control the nanobots here. And can even program the nanobots from across the room." She led me to the computers linked together where Honora, Zara and Goggins were working.

"It's fascinating, Gabe," said Goggins with delight.

Honora shook her head at Goggins. I gathered Honora wasn't taking the same pleasure in coding Stefano's DNA. She had been one of Stefano's prisoners briefly. I was sure she held pity for any prisoner, even Stefano.

Zara was deep in concentration. Her fingers coded faster than I ever saw in the past. I was not sure how Zara felt about experimenting on Stefano. She hated him for what he did to Synthia, forcing her to divulge the whereabouts of rebel leaders, so her coding work, I guessed, was probably payback.

I didn't feel good about any of this. I'd fought Anjori. I knew how strong and smart she was. Becoming a cyborg only made her harder to fight, with increased brain processing speed and the children's gifts embedded in her.

Dr. Rashel took a seat and brought up a picture of Stefano's DNA strands. They were changing and mutating.

"Look, the foreign DNA is binding to his DNA," she said.

I looked at Stefano. His eyelids pulsated back and forth. He opened his eyes. I headed over with Dr. Rashel, and we saw the code cross his pupils.

"The code is uploading. Stefano is now a cyborg," I said, walking away from him. I leaned against one of the lab windows and looked out. I thought about my code now being inside Stefano. "Zara, are you coding all of my program directories to Stefano?" I asked, turning around.

"Yes, all of them. We're guessing that he did that to Anjori and the Mawzians, so we're doing the same," explained Zara.

I was sure that was what Stefano did as well, but that didn't make me feel any more comfortable with the procedure. But the medical and technical support team all seemed to be confident in what they were doing. A nagging question kept coming to my mind.

I leaned over Dr. Rashel. "What exactly did you need me for?"

She took a deep breath. "To fight him."

Dr. Rashel liked to be blunt. She wanted me to fight him? That was crazy. I glanced over to Goggins and Zara, who also seemed surprised.

"I hope it doesn't have to come to that," I said as I turned to Dr. Rashel.

"It has to. That's the only way to see if we've duplicated the directive he gave to the cyborgs. Then we can synthesize a serum of some sort and administer it to him. Then see if he fights you again," she explained. "If he doesn't, then we have a cure."

She seemed to have it all thought out. But mutating DNA strands may not act so predictable in reality.

"My code has mutated. Honora's DNA has mutated. I'm sure so will the cyborgs'," I said.

"Yes, we're aware of that. We'll have to keep Stefano constantly monitored as we adjust the solution," she explained.

"And constantly picking fights with me?" I asked.

"Yes," she said.

"Across the universe while we track down all the Mawzians?"

"Yes, again," she said.

"But there will be hundreds of types of mutations," I said.

"Perhaps, perhaps not," she said.

"It seems impractical," I said.

"Until we find a stable DNA code that we can control, that's the way it has to be. Perhaps we'll get lucky, here, in the lab today," she said.

"Good luck, doctor." I crossed to Goggins at his computer. Every part of me wanted to hop on the *Alyssia* and begin the search for every Mawzian on that ship. I hoped Stoller and Alex were making headway on their return trip to Charbeaux Station. I was ready to put in a comm link to them for a search and destroy mission.

I wasn't as compassionate toward the cybs as Honora. Perhaps she didn't review our shared probability tables that were in the combat directories as to the plethora of bad scenarios the cyborgs could cause in the galaxy.

"We're beginning to code his prime directive," said Zara. We all huddled around her. Dr. Rashel put a call to her comm for more guards to come into the room. Soon after, eight soldiers entered and fanned around Stefano.

I approached Talia and Synthia and put my hands gently on their shoulders. I sent them both a thought. *Sorry to interrupt. Please come back here, behind the guards.* They both emerged out of their meditation and moved behind the guards.

"His file directory will be set up similar to yours, Gabe," said Goggins as he typed away on his keyboard. "There, it's done." He pushed away from his desk. Goggins, Honora, and I headed over to Stefano. His eyes were still open with code running down them.

"Unhook the connections and remove his restraints," ordered Dr. Rashel. The med techs removed the computer connection wires and released the straps around Stefano.

"I need to set the password," said Honora as she jumped back to her desk.

The lab doors suddenly opened, and two Oliverian marines surveyed the room. They made a waving motion, and Swina, Jazar and General Foxwell entered.

As soon as Foxwell saw us, he stopped. "What the blazes are they doing here?"

No other Heragi military personnel were with them. Swina and Jazar must have done a very good job convincing Foxwell they were friendly and trustworthy enough to come into the room with no backup.

Swina strode up to her sister, on the center table next to Stefano. "I believe you know of my sister, Anjori. Recently rescued from a Mawzian prison by these friends." She waved her hands toward us.

Foxwell took two steps forward. The look on his face hardened. He glanced at Anjori and then saw Stefano. "What are you doing to him? Release him immediately," growled Foxwell.

Swina was not swayed or fearful, I found, as I checked her bio-metrics. She was steady, much like the warrior her sister was. Or perhaps all Oliverians were as strong as them.

Swina motioned to her marines. They grabbed Foxwell and restrained him. "You will be a witness to the experiments that you instructed Stefano himself to conduct on my sister and the Mawzians," she said with authority.

"You won't get away with this," threatened Foxwell. "We were offering an alliance, but that is off the table. You're now an enemy of the Heragi Empire."

Stefano began to awaken.

He lunged toward Swina.

I stepped forward to stop him. He had seized Swina's throat. I hit Stefano from behind which doubled him over and pulled Swina away from him.

We squared off.

This wasn't the Stefano I had met weeks ago on the planet Suissey. He was strong and confident. He came at me with a right hook and then swung a cart up into my chest. I didn't want to hurt him. I just took his punches, thinking he could be worn down.

The marines hustled Swina out of the room, but Foxwell was kept inside with us.

"Didn't you set a trigger word?" Goggins asked Honora.

"I did. It's the word *Heragi*," Honora replied.

"Stop him," yelled Dr. Rashel to Zara and Goggins.

"We're trying," yelled Zara as they sifted through Stefano's long code files.

"Go after them, Stefano. They are enemies of the Heragi Empire and should be annihilated," Foxwell yelled at the newly created cyborg. "Kill the robot first."

"Get Foxwell out of here," said Dr. Rashel to the remaining guards. They pulled Foxwell through the door.

I tried to lure Stefano away from the others to the other side of the room. "How does it feel? To be a guinea pig?"

"Not so bad. In fact, I never felt so good," he replied as he sent a right uppercut flying toward my chin. I took it. He was strong.

"How are we doing?" I yelled back to the coding team.

"Almost there," Goggins replied.

"We're going to find those Mawzians and stop your little cyborg army," I said.

"And how do you plan to do that?" he asked with a smirk.

"Change their prime directives," I said.

"Every living thing needs a prime directive. Even a robot,"

he said. Then he came at me with a leg kick to my chest. It flung me to the wall, and he pummeled my head with a chair. He turned and ran for the door. I pulled out my gun. It was on kill phase. I pointed it at Stefano's back. He grabbed the door handle.

"No, don't shoot him," yelled Dr. Rashel.

"Got it!" cried Zara.

"Prime directive deleted!" said Goggins.

Stefano turned the handle and then crumpled to the ground. I holstered my gun and ran over to him and lifted him off the ground. I took him to the table and laid him out. Dr. Rashel and her techs swarmed over to monitor him.

Dr. Rashel said, "He's flatlining!"

Her med techs tried to revive him. They stopped after thirty minutes.

We all circled his table.

"What happened?" asked Honora.

"I don't know. Zara and I just re-coded his prime directive so he would stop attacking," said Goggins.

"But what *exactly* did you do?" I asked. "What did you change the prime directive *to*?"

"We didn't change it. We *deleted* it," said Zara. She sat down, looking over Stefano's code as it flashed down her screen.

I moved over to the window and looked over the beautiful city of Yusses.

"What? What did we do? We didn't mean to kill him," said Goggins as he backed up against a wall. He was scared. He didn't want any blame. And I didn't want to blame anyone in the room. If only we had taken out that ship of Mawzians — and then Anjori.

My mind shifted back to the matter at hand in the lab. We'd all had a hand in killing a man, bad as he was.

When I had seen and witnessed Stefano's cruelty and horrible manipulations of Heragi rebels, I would have welcomed his death, even if it was at my hands. But this didn't feel right.

Perhaps because now, we had fewer options, or maybe it was because his death seemed to make us no better than him.

I turned around to face everyone.

The door opened. I was expecting Swina and her marines to walk into the room to see the mess we had created. But it wasn't Swina. It was Ava and Damiel Kell.

Honora and Talia ran over to their parents and wrapped their arms around them. There was a sudden pain in my heart. I'd felt that pain before though and pushed it aside.

"He needed a prime directive," I said.

Ava positioned herself in the middle of the room. "Correct, Gabe. All living things need a prime directive — or they die."

16

Ava and Damiel looked around the room.

"Where is Alex?" asked Damiel.

"He left," said Honora.

"Left? Where did he go?" asked Ava.

"To a substation called Charbeaux. He's helping stop the spread of the Mawzian cyborgs," I said.

Ava gently placed her daughters in her husband's arms and marched over to me. "You let him go alone?"

"No," I said, trying to sound like her son leaving was quite reasonable. Only it wasn't. "He left with a pilot we met there, who helped us rescue Synthia."

"Do you even remember your prime directive?" she seethed.

"Yes, to protect the children," I said. "That will always be my prime directive."

"Then how could you let him go?" She stepped closer to me.

"My prime directive does not include keeping your children prisoners. I protect them when they are with me, to the best of my ability," I explained.

"It should be more than that," she said as she spun around.

"I would lay down my life for them and kill anyone who

would harm them," I said. "But I will not stop them from living. They're not hostages."

Ava stopped.

I hit a nerve.

"They would be safe on Zaradorba," she said.

"No, Mom. Gabe's right. You can't protect us from everything. We have to stop the Heragi Empire," said Honora.

Talia signed to her mother, *Mom, with our gifts, we may be able to win.*

Ava hugged Talia, who signed again, *Maybe that is why we were born.*

Damiel embraced Talia. "Yes, we need to let them fight, Ava."

Ava nodded, holding back tears.

"How can we help?" asked Damiel.

Dr. Rashel stepped forward. "Ava and Damiel, thank you for coming." She shook their hands and brought them to the tables holding Stefano and Anjori. "I'm glad our comms team was able to contact you on Zaradorba."

"It looks like we were too late to help you with him," said Damiel, pointing to Stefano.

"Yes, I'm sorry, too," said Dr. Rashel. She pointed to the other operating table. "This is Anjori. She is Swina's sister."

"Please show me your data," said Ava.

"Here, over here," said Goggins. He got out of his seat and offered it to Ava. Zara got up as well, and Damiel looked at their code. The husband and wife team discussed what they saw in the code. Damiel stood up and addressed us.

"You all did an excellent job. But it is what Ava and I suspected. The prime directive needs to be replaced, not just deleted. That is what killed Stefano. But of course, even if you change the prime directive, it will not stop the gifts and programs that are in the cyborgs' DNA from our children and Gabe's code," said Damiel.

"You mean Anjori and the Mawzians who were made into cyborgs will always have that DNA and Gabe's code, and we can't figure out some cure or untangle it from their own DNA?" asked Dr. Rashel.

"Correct," said Damiel. "If it is even possible, it would take years of computation and testing."

"What are other ramifications of this?" asked Dr. Rashel.

Ava got up and looked over the gold city. She touched the back of her neck. "Let me think — for starters, their DNA and gifts can be passed down to their children. They and their children could be used by the Heragi Empire to create havoc."

"They could imprison them and use them like they did to me on Suissey," said Synthia. "I was forced to break into the minds of rebel leaders and inform Stefano when people were lying to him to see where their moles were hidden in the Heragi government."

Synthia rose from her seat. "That should not be wished or condemned on another soul," she said. "It's not the gift of telepathy that is bad. It's the possible imprisonment of the people who have the gifts."

"Telepathy from Talia, my self-healing and kinesiology from Alex," said Honora.

Zara said, "And with Gabe's code, they have advanced fighting and piloting skills, and the Heragis can give them any prime directive they want."

"And they will be mission capable. They can be programmed to put their lives last, to self-sacrifice, even if it's against their own will or morals," said Goggins as he paced the room.

Then Talia held up her arm comm. "Are these cybs related to us? They share our DNA. It came from us."

Everyone was silent.

Damiel got on his knee to look his youngest in the eye. "You're intertwined."

"I don't want to kill them," said Talia through her transceiver.

"That's why we're here, Talia," said Ava. "We will find a way. A different way. We'll recode Anjori's prime directive."

"And figure out a way to get it to the Mawzians," said Damiel.

Dr. Rashel grabbed a small bottle and handed it to Zara. "These are nanobots. Once you find the cyborgs, you need to inject them with these. Then control them externally with the coding that the Kells and I will send you."

"Got it," said Zara.

"If we can even find the cybs," said Goggins, scratching his head. "They could be scattered out in the galaxy."

"That's why we need to leave now," I said. "When Ava and Damiel have the code, they can send it to us. But we have to go help Stoller and Alex find the Mawzians."

Zara and Goggins nodded.

"Copy that," said Zara. She started walking out.

"Agreed," said Goggins. "The Kells were always better than me at coding." He smiled and started for the door.

"Synthia?" asked Zara as she noticed her old friend wasn't following her.

Synthia sat down. "I need to stay here and help Anjori."

Zara returned, and they embraced. "I'll be back for you."

Synthia kissed her friend on the cheek. "I know you will. And thank you for always finding me."

"I'm coming with you," said Honora as she ran to me.

Talia also ran to me.

"Honora, Talia. You can't —" Ava started and then she stopped herself and put her head down. "You would just steal another ship and run away, right?"

"Yes," said Honora. She and Talia ran back to their parents and hugged them goodbye.

I headed toward the door.

"Gabe," said Ava.

I turned around to face her.

"Thank you," she said as Damiel put his arm around her waist.

"You're welcome. You're always welcome," I said. Then I stopped. I remembered something. "Where is Jebediah?"

Damiel said, "He's trying to rescue any remaining rebels off Heragi. He was trying to make it to the Hiraxi Moon Station without being detected. He has friends there."

Hiraxi. Interesting choice. It was one of four moons in the gravitational orbit of a planet near Heragi called Putari.

I nodded and walked out the door with my team.

Back on the *Alyssia*, everyone settled into their seats and buckled up. Honora took the co-commander seat across from me. I watched her prep for launch. A warm feeling started in my chest. It was good to see her there.

Zara helped Goggins latch into his seat. Talia had her cici-chimp and was holding it tight.

"Feti, prepare us for launch," I said.

"Affirmative, Gabe," it said.

I started the engines, and Feti closed our doors and retracted the ramp. We received clearance from the planet-port tower and pulled out of the city of Yusses. We all watched as the city of gold became smaller in our window. We left their atmosphere with a g-force that pushed us back into our seats. Then we were out in the darkness, and the stars appeared.

"Where are we headed, Gabe?" asked Feti.

"Back to Charbeaux Station," I said. "When will we come into live comm capability with the station?"

"Within eight hours," Feti said.

"Thank you. I'll want a link with Stoller's ship which should be gated there. It's called the *Ravena*."

"Copy that, Gabe," it said.

We navigated back onto the Karakova Highway with the mapping that Goggins made us from our last trip. Everyone unbuckled and went to the galley for a meal that Feti had prepared for them. They asked me to join, but I declined, making up an excuse that some system logs needed review. They may have known I was fibbing, but I wanted alone time to work out the strategic probabilities of the Mawzian cybs.

I hoped Stoller's friends at the station were able to detain or at least slow down the Mawzian ship at their gates. If the Kells could get us a coding solution for the cybs' prime directive, then we could round them up there at the station. But if the cybs had already dispersed, then we'd have to divide up the galaxy and begin a massive search. I was hoping for the former option.

I should have demanded to interrogate Foxwell while I was still on Oliveria. Knowing the Heragi plan for the cybs would be helpful, especially if they had already spread out to other planets.

While I was thinking of different scenarios, which all seemed unpleasant, Feti interrupted me. "Gabe?"

"Yes, Feti," I answered.

"I missed you," it said.

I stopped and lifted my head. "I missed you, too. But we weren't gone too long on Oliveria."

"I'm listening to the conversation in the galley. It sounds like you were in another awful fight. And this time with that Stefano person," it said.

My chest began to hurt. I felt bad for Feti. He was attaching to me emotionally, and I didn't think that was wise of it, especially with the state of the galaxy, and plus, I had my own problems.

"Yes, we fought. I just defended myself, really," I explained.

"What if you get hurt, really hurt?" said Feti. "How will I know?"

He had a point. I wasn't including or communicating with

Feti enough. He was a part of our team.

"I'm sorry, Feti. I will keep you more informed. I promise."

"Okay, Gabe. Thank you.".

"And if I get hurt, I will let you know, okay?"

"Okay. Because, you know, I may be able to help you."

"Yes, you may."

I let some time go by as I looked over the Karakova Highway. The lights that encompassed it and the harmonics that powered it were beautiful.

With my own power supply being enabled by harmonics, it somehow felt like home to me. And I can't even describe what home feels like. I guess it feels like the lab where I was created. Where I first heard and then saw Ava and Damiel and even Goggins. But this highway felt even better. It felt wide open, yet contained, and it felt like it could take care of me.

"This highway is beautiful," said Feti. "Life is good on the Karakova Highway. Isn't it, Gabe?"

"Yes, it is a sight to behold," I said.

Purple, blue and yellow-green bounced off all the transport ships we passed. I wondered where they were all headed with their goods, being navigated by other systems like Feti.

"I'm glad we can be here alone, just us two."

I grunted a laugh. "Yes, maybe there'll be a time when we aren't chasing or rescuing someone. When we can just go for a ride."

"A trip," said Feti with some excitement.

"Yes, a trip. A vacation."

I continued to look out on the bouncing lights of the highway with Feti.

When the team awoke from their brief sleep, they took their seats on the bridge.

"Gabe, we're within comm range of Charbeaux Station. I

will link with the *Ravena*'s comm system. One moment please," said Feti.

"Thank you," I replied.

"Do you think they detained the Mawzians?" asked Honora.

"We'll soon find out," said Goggins as he worked on the comms with Feti.

"We have audio only. Go ahead, Gabe," said Feti.

"Stoller, this is Gabe. Do you copy?"

Silence.

"Stoller? Alex? This is Gabe. Do you copy?"

"Gabe, this is Alex. It's good to hear your voice," he said.

"Hey, Alex. Where's Stoller?" I asked.

"He's right here. He's just waking up," said Alex.

"Waking up?" I asked.

"Yeah, he got knocked out by Uncle Jeb. They were playing quinker, and Stoller tried to explain more quinker rules and take Uncle Jeb's ship in a big win," said Alex.

Honora and Talia started to laugh.

"Jiminy, we've got a spaceship full of cybs that could infect the whole galaxy with prime directive death sentences, and those two are playing cards and slugging it out?" said Goggins. He dragged his hands through his hair, making it stand straight up.

"We're landing soon and will come visit you on the *Ravena*," I said.

"Not soon enough. Over and out," said Alex.

We received our clearance for landing from the port master at Charbeaux Station and docked near the *Ravena*. We passed by a gate or two down in the planet-port and marched up its ramp.

We headed toward the bridge, but when we were nearing the galley, we heard voices. We walked in and saw Stoller with a bleeding nose that Alex was tending to, and there stood Jebediah Kell with bloody knuckles.

Zara stepped forward. "What the heck is going on here?"

"We do have a shipload of cyborgs we need to stop, right? Or has that changed?" asked Goggins with a bit of gravitas I didn't know was inside of him.

"Really? A fist-fight?" I said.

Honora and Talia went to their Uncle Jeb and Alex and hugged them warmly. I guess they weren't as annoyed.

"Calm down, everyone," said Stoller. "The cybs are hovering on the other side of the planet. I had my planet-port buddies here give them the runaround about the station gates being all booked up. They've been hanging in space for over a sol."

"So, you've just been, what? Playing quinker and let me guess — drinking gin?" asked Zara as she took a seat at the table.

"No, I ran out of gin eight hours ago," said Stoller.

"Actually, Zara, we've been monitoring them and getting agreements from Charbeaux Station pilots to help us when and if it gets ugly down here," said Alex.

"Even though many of these pilots have no problem with the Heragi Empire," added Stoller. "They're sticking their necks out, for us." He pointed his thumb to his chest for emphasis.

"For you," said Jebediah.

"Yeah, I guess," said Stoller as he wiped his bloody nose. "How did it go back on Oliveria? Did you cure Anjori?"

No one wanted to talk first. It got awkward, so I began. "No, not yet. Ava and Damiel Kell arrived, and they took over the work with Dr. Rashel and Synthia."

"Are they close? To a cure? How are we going to stop the Mawzians if we aren't going to kill them? Or has that changed?" asked Stoller.

"No, that's not changed," said Honora.

"Things got complicated on Oliveria." Goggins sat down.

"How complicated?" asked Jeb.

"Our first attempt at a solution didn't work out," said Zara as she looked out the galley window.

"Did you hurt Anjori?" asked Stoller.

"No. Stefano was the one we ended up testing on. He died. We messed up," said Goggins.

Stoller raised his eyebrows in surprise but didn't say anything.

"Stefano's dead?" said Jeb. "No loss there if it got you closer to a solution."

"Jeb, that doesn't help," said Zara.

"He's the reason why we're all here," defended Jeb. "I'm not going to apologize for what I said." He turned to the children. "Call me a son of a gun, but we need a solution to this. It could go bad every way you can imagine."

I wanted to interject, but I didn't. What could I add about Stefano? What was done was done. But even that rationalization didn't sit well with me.

A comm link came through into the galley. "Stoller, this is Leroy. The Mawzian ship is landing. Three gates away from you."

"Copy that. Thanks, Leroy," said Stoller. "Ding-dong, guess who's coming to dinner?"

Everyone got up.

"What's the plan?" asked Zara.

"We need to detain them," said Jeb.

"Until the code gets here from the Kells, apparently," said Stoller, grabbing his gun.

"And there's one more thing we need to tell you about," said Zara. She took out the bottle of nanobots and shook them in the small jar.

"What the heck are those?" asked Stoller.

Zara smiled as she handed the jar to him.

He tried to see the nanobots as he squinted and held the jar up to the light.

17

———————

"So, let me see if I understand this," said Stoller as he paced around the bridge of his ship. "We need to detain the Mawzians on their ship and not kill them, even though they have advanced fighting skills now built into their DNA."

"Don't forget about advanced weapons training programs," added Goggins.

"Thanks for the reminder, Doc. And they also have ancient powers from the Kell kids. We have to inject them with nanobots and then wait on the Kell scientists to send us code to stop their killer instinct to wipe out any humanoid or alien that doesn't agree with the Heragi Empire." He stopped and dropped into his commander pilot seat. "Did I miss anything else?"

"Uh, yes, they have the expert pilot programs that Gabe has, that now they have, that you failed to mention," said Goggins as he thought and scratched his head, remembering.

Stoller shot Goggins a look which could have struck down a spaceship.

"You basically got it," said Goggins.

"You need to get physically close to the Mawzians," said Zara as she held up the bottle of nanobots. She took out two silver injection devices. "Here, take these. Every Mawzian needs one shot that has nanobots in it."

Stoller took the devices and put them in his jacket. "Where do I need to give them the shot?"

"Anywhere. The nanobots just have to get into their blood stream," said Zara.

"Great," said Stoller. Zara touched his arm gently and squeezed it. They locked eyes for a moment. "If anything happens to me, you can have my gin supply."

"Gee, thanks," she replied.

He grinned and said, "You have no idea how much that gin means to me."

"I think I can guess."

Jeb inserted himself between Stoller and Zara. "No one is going to have to bequeath gin or anything to anybody. Now how do the cybs identify an enemy of the Heragi empire?" He looked around the bridge. "Does anyone know?"

"We think they have already been programmed with known rebel names and planets that have resisters like Zaradorba," said Zara.

"Who on this bridge is not on the list?" asked Stoller.

Zara and Goggins looked around. Jebediah was certainly on the list along with the Kell children. And of course, Zara and Goggins. Me, yes, the rogue robot that saved the Kell children, would be on the list as well. So, that left only one person on the bridge.

Goggins stated the obvious. "Just you, Stoller. You're off the radar. Stefano probably never heard of you or knew you once fought alongside Anjori."

"That's right," said Jeb. "In fact, the Heragi never considered the Oliverians or Deragians as enemies. Experimenting on Anjori was really just out of convenience. Not a declaration of war against the Oliverian planet."

"I was afraid of that," said Stoller as he pulled a bottle of gin out from under his navigation console and took a swig.

Footsteps approached the bridge. I stood up and pulled out my gun. Everyone ducked except Jeb who also pulled out his side arm and Stoller who took another swig of gin.

"Whoa, whoa, there robot — jumping jet streams!" yelled a man in a Charbeaux Station utility uniform.

"Put your weapon down, Gabe. You don't want to blow the head off the man who's going to help us save the galaxy, do you?" said Stoller. "This is my friend Leroy, the station's planet-port manager."

I lowered my gun and Jebediah followed suit.

"Nice to meet you, Leroy," I said.

"You all need to chill out. You're way too jumpy, and that makes me jumpy, and I don't like to be jumpy," said Leroy.

"Leroy, Leroy. Sit down. Have a drink," said Stoller as he pulled out a shot glass from underneath his navigational console.

Zara rolled her eyes.

"What? I don't have room for a legit bar," said Stoller.

"I didn't say anything," she said.

"You didn't have to," snapped Stoller. He handed Leroy a shot which he drank in a gulp.

"Stoller, listen. I don't want to get wrapped up in your old marine galaxy fighting melodramatics. This is the Charbeaux Station, and we have gladly been a neutral landing zone for two hundred years for any pirate, scoundrel, thief, outlaw or rebel who wants to visit our quaint domicile and trading post. To put it bluntly, we don't judge," explained Leroy.

Stoller poured Leroy another shot.

"It doesn't feel right keeping these Mawzians in their ship when they've done no harm to me or anyone at this station. Do you hear me?" Leroy took off his cap and wiped a handkerchief over his damp forehead.

"Yes, yes, I hear you. And thank you for explaining this to

me and my friends. But Leroy, we need your help. I need your help. And you may not have signed up for this but you've being drafted, buddy boy." Stoller pulled up his arm comm and showed a few pics to Leroy.

Leroy's eyes almost popped out of his head. "You're blackmailing me? You really are low."

"Sorry, but would you have agreed to help me more if I hadn't?" asked Stoller.

"No," said Leroy.

"So, you see. I had to do it. Don't hold it against me," said Stoller with a smile.

Leroy shook his head and held up his hands. "Fine."

I guess they were friends. A funny sort of friendship, but I didn't care. We needed Leroy to help us, and Stoller convinced him, rather improperly, to help us.

Stoller slapped his hands together and stood up. "Okay, me and Leroy will greet the Mawzians and assist them with their supply needs. We'll try to get some intel and then we just need that code from the Kells. Sound good?"

"That sounds like a very basic plan. Many things could go wrong," I said.

"What? What did the robot say?" said Leroy.

"My name is Gabe."

"Okay. What did Gabe say? I don't like when things go wrong. That sounds dangerous."

"Alex, the ship is yours," said Stoller. "Until I get back."

"Copy that. Don't worry, I won't lose it in a card game."

"Come on, Leroy. This will give you a story to repeat a thousand times at the Blue Edger bar," said Stoller as he left the bridge. Leroy trailed him, complaining the whole way down the hallway.

"We need your body cam on, Stoller," I shouted.

"Copy that," yelled Stoller.

Jeb turned to me. "I heard you rescued Synthia on Mawzi."

"Yes, she stayed back with the Kells on Oliveria," I said. "And they have Foxwell, too."

"How did that happen?" asked Jeb.

"The Heragi were trying to make an alliance with the Oliveria Providence," I explained. "But it didn't go the way Foxwell would have liked it to."

"Huh," said Jeb as he rubbed the back of his neck and thought.

"Jeb, Synthia didn't give up any rebel leader names when she was held captive on Mawzi. Stefano didn't use her like that. I just wanted you to know," said Zara. "That's what you were wondering, right?"

"Yeah, it was. How was he using her?"

"She was there to break into the mind of Anjori and the Mawzians, to make sure his experiments were taking," explained Zara.

Jeb shook his head. "It's still dangerous."

"What's dangerous?" said Honora.

"Having Synthia out there," said Jeb.

"You could say that about me too. And Alex, Talia, or Gabe," said Honora as she got heated up. "What do you want to do? Lock us up?"

"Honora, if you want to play with the adults, then you need to start acting like one," said Jeb.

"Cut it out," said Zara, jumping up.

"Act like an adult? Act more like you? Adults started all this crap. I'm going back to the *Alyssia*." Honora stormed out.

Talia gave her uncle a stern look and held up her arm comm "Don't ever talk to her like that again." Jeb put up his hands in frustration. Talia ran after her sister.

"Sorry. Honora? Talia? Come back!" yelled Jeb.

"Nice job. Way to alienate your family," said Zara.

"Guys, now that you've broken up our family reunion, take a look at this. We have a problem," said Alex. He pointed to his monitor. Zara, Jeb and I leaned over. "Leroy gave us access to monitor the station's planet-port gates. A Heragi ship is landing next to the Mawzian ship."

"Contact Stoller," said Jeb.

"He's already in their gate area," Alex said as he opened up the ship's comm to link directly to Stoller's arm comm. "Stoller? Stoller?"

"Yeah, kid?" asked Stoller. "Make it quick. I'm walking up the Mawzians' ramp right now."

"A Heragi ship has just landed at the gate next door to the Mawzians. Expect company," said Alex.

"And turn on your chest cam. Keep your audio open," I said, leaning into the comms.

"Sorry, forgot, Gabe," said Stoller.

His chest cam image came up on multiple screens on the *Ravena*'s navigation deck for all of us to watch. He turned, and we saw him and Leroy entering the airlock chamber of the Mawzian ship. Leroy looked nervous.

Two male Mawzians greeted them as they passed through the airlock chamber into the main hull.

"Hello, I'm Leroy. We talked a few times." He looked around the room at all the Mawzians surrounding them.

The bigger of the two Mawzian males approached them. "What's his name?"

"Him? He's Rafe," said Leroy, pointing to Stoller. "He's our planet-port's med tech."

"Howdy," said Stoller.

"Why were we forced to anchor off-planet for so long? We saw ships come and go from here," complained the large Mawzian.

"We apologize," said Stoller. "Those ships had reservations ahead of you, and we were at capacity since we have a virus outbreak. It's bad." He nudged Leroy's arm.

"Yeah, virus. It's a bad one," emphasized Leroy.

"I'm afraid we're going to have to vaccinate everyone," Stoller said as he pulled out the injectable shot device. "Uh, what's your name?"

The lead Mawzian said, "Vincent."

"Okay, Vincent. How many folks do we have onboard here?" said Stoller as he pretended to prep the device.

"Twenty," said Vincent. "And one child."

"Okay, please line up, and we'll get you all vaccinated, and then Leroy and I can even escort you around the station to make sure you have all the supplies you need for your journey."

Leroy proceeded to step in front of everyone. "Yes. Please line up, everyone. One line. Thank you."

Stoller smiled as he gave Vincent the first shot. "There you go, sir. Thank you." Vincent left, and the next Mawzian walked up and took their shot, then the next.

"A vaccine," said Zara. "Brilliant."

We watched as Stoller continued giving the shots to the lined up Mawzians.

The last person in line was a woman who held the hand of a small girl.

"That's the woman Honora bought on Mawzi. Her name is Meeor," I said.

"She has a child," said Jeb.

"Yes, her name is Belin. They were initially the reason Honora stole that ship. To save them," I explained.

"Hello," said Stoller to Meeor. He gave her the shot. "And who do we have here?"

Belin smiled at Stoller. Meeor then pulled Belin behind her. "No, she can't have the shot. She has a compromised immune system."

Stoller stopped. "This is a very safe vaccine."

"No. I said no." Belin started to back away. Stoller stepped toward the child with the shot but Vincent stepped in.

"The lady said no. Got it?" Vincent towered over Stoller. Leroy got in between them.

"Fine, that's okay. She'll just have to stay on the ship, um, quarantined in her cabin," said Leroy.

Vincent nodded and motioned for Belin and Meeor to go back to their sleeping bays.

"The rest of our crew would enjoy stretching their legs on the station," said Vincent.

"Sure, follow us," said Leroy. He and Stoller led the Mazwians off the ship and onto the station.

Stoller got a bit in front of the crowd and spoke into his cam. "Sorry, we couldn't get the small girl."

"That's okay, we'll worry about her later," said Jeb.

"I'll keep in contact," said Stoller.

"Copy that," said Alex.

"What do you think that Heragi ship is doing here?" asked Goggins.

Alex typed into his console and brought up the Charbeaux travel logs. "It's not just any Heragi ship. It's Foxwell's ship the *Firestone*."

"What? I thought he was captured on Oliveria?" said Jeb as he spun around to me.

"Foxwell was there. We saw him. And we saw his ship was there at the gate when we left. Maybe his crew escaped," I said.

"Dammit, Gabe. You should have disabled his ship," shouted Jeb. "And killed Foxwell."

"Is that all you are trained to do? Kill?" hissed Zara. "That wasn't Gabe's or our call to kill Foxwell. And the Oliverians wouldn't have just stepped aside for us to do that."

"I think they were planning on using him as a bargaining chip," added Goggins.

"Walk it off, Jeb," I said. "Zara and the children are right. Maybe there's a better way out of this than just killing everyone who opposes us."

Jeb headed for the door. He was hot and ready to blow. His bio-levels were skyrocketing. He turned around to face us. "When will you all grow up? And do you think that is what Anjori will want when she gets cured? To show them mercy, when they experimented on her and turned her into you, Gabe?"

Ouch. That last one stung.

"Alex, send me the link to Stoller's comms," said Jeb.

"Where are you going?" asked Zara.

"I'll be tailing Stoller. We can't risk these Mawzians splitting up and taking transports all over the galaxy. Are you coming or not?"

Zara looked at me and Goggins.

"Yes, I'm coming with you," I said. "Alex, you stay here with the ship. Keep an eye on the Mawzian ship and any activity."

"Copy that, Gabe," said Alex.

"Zara and Goggins, go back to the *Alyssia*. Honora and Talia should be there by now. When that code comes in from the Kells, we will need to upload it to all the Mawzians," I told them.

"On our way," said Zara, who left the bridge.

"You don't have to tell me twice to get out of harm's way," said Goggins. And there was never a truer statement than that.

"And, Alex, make sure the woman, Meeor, and her child don't leave the ship," I said. "They can't leave this substation. Especially the girl Belin."

"Copy that," said Alex.

I left the *Ravena* and followed Jeb onto the substation, following the route Stoller and Leroy took with the Mawzians.

18

Jeb and I entered the Charbeaux Station main tunnel from the planet-port, making sure we weren't detectable by the Mawzian group.

"How far back do you think their sensors can pick up on their most wanted list?" asked Jeb.

"They received that code from me. My eyesight has facial recognition up to fifty yards, and they most likely have security shots of all of us along with an alien directory. They can discern a Heragi from an Oliverian, for example," I explained.

We exited the tunnel and merged into the crowd. I looked up to the multi-level substation and was still in awe of its magnitude.

I saw the group of Mawzians with their heads looking upward also. They must have been just as amazed as any first or second-time visitor to the Charbeaux Station. This was even more amazing considering they weren't using their eyes but utilizing the vibrations that allowed them to see, that Stefano must have perfected.

"Look, there they are," I said, nodding ahead of us.

Jeb grunted. "Looks like they haven't gotten out much."

"They're underground dwellers. Many of them have never been out of the tunnels of Mawzi, I suspect," I said.

"And now they're slaves of the Heragi Empire. No, but it's worse than that. They're cyborgs with killing orders," he said.

Stoller and Leroy were letting the Mawzians look at the stores and vendors, probably agreeing that stalling was the best we could do right now as we waited for the code relay from the Kells back on Oliveria.

We watched from a block away. A group of vendors tried to sell their wares to us. Jeb brushed them off, and we continued our slow tracking behind the Mawzians.

"I certainly hope there's no Heragi rebels stopping here," said Jeb.

He had a good point. For the past fifty years, I was sure the enemy list of Heragi had grown to be long, and there was no reason Foxwell and Stefano wouldn't have loaded the whole extensive list. And they would be able to have that list updated constantly as their Mawzian cybs traveled the galaxy.

"Stoller, Gabe, I've got cams on the Heragi ship. Two soldiers just left. They look like they're headed for the main tunnel into the station."

"Copy that," I said.

"Blasters," said Stoller. "Gabe, where are you?"

"Fifty-five yards behind you," I replied.

"Okay, stay close," said Stoller.

"That's as close as Jeb and I can get right now without being detected," I explained.

"Copy that," said Stoller.

I watched as Vincent looked like he received a comm through an implanted ear device. He touched his ear.

"Gabe, do you see that? Vincent is getting some comm. He's stopping his group," said Stoller. "I'll try to get them moving."

Stoller raised his arms and tried to usher them over to a

wares store for food supplies. Vincent declined and wasn't budging.

"They've stopped moving," said Jeb as he looked ahead. "Those Heragi soldiers must be giving them instructions."

"We need to stop those soldiers," I said. "They're going to be coming up behind us." I turned around to get a look at visitors coming into the station from the planet-port. I saw the two Heragi soldiers. They headed toward the Mawzians.

Then Leroy passed us and popped right in front of the soldiers, halting them with his planet-port identification badge.

"What is Leroy doing?" muttered Jeb under his breath.

"Being a hero," said Stoller, watching his friend risk his life.

"He's detaining them," I said.

Leroy was trying to redirect the soldiers back into the tunnel, back to the planet-port. I had no idea what excuse he was giving them — citations, permits or even the virus excuse. The soldiers were shaking their heads and not having any of it from Leroy. They stunned him with one shot. Leroy withered to the ground.

"Man down," yelled Jeb into his comm.

One of the soldiers spoke into his arm comm. He must be giving more direction to Vincent. Vincent touched his ear. It was an instinctive move and took practice to not touch your ear when you heard a voice pop in.

"Blazes, Leroy. The Mawzians are dispersing. I need extra eyes here," said Stoller, who began to walk away as the soldiers followed in his direction. Stoller disappeared into the crowd.

People surrounded Leroy and helped the fallen man. He was alive and only disabled for a short time. A med tech team rushed to him.

Alex broke into the comm. "Honora and Talia are on their way to help track the Mawzians."

"Copy that," said Stoller.

"Honora, Talia? Can you hear me?" I asked.

"Copy that, Gabe. We're just entering the tunnel," said Honora.

"Keep more than fifty yards back, or you'll be detected," I ordered them.

"Got it," said Honora.

"Get to the fourth floor, Honora. I see five are on that level. I'll be going to the tenth. I think there are three on that floor," said Stoller.

"I got eyes on two heading to the pavilion area," said Jeb. "How many does that make we have accounted for?"

"That's ten. Nine are unaccounted for," I replied. "Zara, can you put a tracking system on their nanobots?"

"Working on that right now, Gabe. I need a few minutes," said Zara.

"I picked up four on the eleventh floor," I said. "That means we have five unaccounted for."

"We don't have a few minutes, Zara. They're probably headed to private spaceship gates. They're positioned all over the station. The wealthier class here gets special clearance and pays a pretty penny for it," said Stoller.

"Goggins is headed out to find the missing five," said Zara.

"I think those five are on level thirty-six," said Stoller.

"Copy that," said Goggins.

"Who's got eyes on the soldiers?" asked Stoller.

No one answered.

"Blasters," said Stoller.

"I got 'em. They showed up on the cams covering the Mawzian ship. They're boarding it," said Alex.

"They're going to take the woman and the girl," I said.

"You mean the girl without a nanobot," said Jeb with annoyance in his voice. "What exactly do you want us to do if these Mawzians, and let us not forget they are weaponized to be killer cyborgs, steal some personal spacecraft and zoom off into the Edge?"

Silence.

There was nothing we could do.

These cybs could out fight us, split open our minds, and self-heal if we hurt them.

"Jeb, stand down!" I yelled. "Stand down!"

"What?" said Jeb. "No way."

I ran down the escalator stairs to the pavilion area where Jeb was tracking his Mawzians.

"Stop, Jeb. I'm coming down for you," I yelled. "Everyone back to the *Alyssia* and the *Ravena*."

"Copy that," said Goggins.

"Standing down," said Stoller. "Blasted."

"Talia and I are on our way to the *Alyssia*," said Honora.

"Gabe, those Heragi soldiers have taken the woman and child. They are boarding them on their Heragi ship," Alex reported.

"Copy that," I said.

I charged into the Pavilion, and Jeb was already in a heated fight with the two Mawzians he'd been following. He'd smashed one with a trash can and had one pinned down with a bench. Residents and visitors to the Charbeaux Station may look the other way to the many fights that happened in the alleyways of their community, but this was drawing a circle of spectators. Most likely because the two Mawzians were still dressed like slaves and one was a woman who was fighting pretty well against the buff Jebediah Kell.

The woman Mawzian had the moves of a fighting warrior down to an expert level. In six swift moves, she had Jebediah pinned down and could have easily snapped his neck if I hadn't distracted her. The male Mawzian threw the bench that previously pinned him down at me. And he threw it with his mind, not his arms.

The growing crowd gave an audible gasp when they saw his telekinesis skills. I caught the bench and threw it back. It hit his head and cut him deeply. That cut should have bled him out, but he placed his hand to his head and self-healed in seconds.

I needed to get Jeb out of here. I grabbed him by his shirt collar. "We are exiting now, General."

Jeb kicked and yelled, but I didn't let go until he stopped squirming. We had to run at full throttle and dodge through the street vendors to escape the Mawzians. By then they had identified our facial features in their Heragi Most Wanted list.

We made it to the tunnel leading to the planet-port, and I got on my comm to the *Alyssia*. "Feti, begin launch procedures," I called.

"Gabe, this is Honora. I already got them going."

"Thank you. Be there shortly," I said.

"I'm heading to my ship," yelled Jeb.

"Stoller, Alex? Are you lifting off?" I said into my comm.

"Yes, affirmative. We're on the tail of the Heragi ship," said Stoller.

I ran up the ramp of the *Alyssia* and onto the bridge. I looked around and saw Goggins, Zara and Talia. Everyone was strapped in. I took the commander's seat and turned around. "Where is Honora?" I asked.

"She ran in and then ran out. She's taking over the Mawzian ship," said Zara.

"We tried to stop her but you know Honora," said a flustered Goggins.

Talia held up her arm comm "She flew that ship once. She can fly it again. We will need the extra air power."

I strapped in and started lifting off.

She was right. We would need the extra air power. The *Alyssia* lifted over the Charbeaux Station.

"Goggins, where is everyone?" I asked.

Goggins reviewed the ship's navigation screen with Zara. They had the nanobot tracker on a second screen.

"Let's merge the spaceship tracker with the nanobot tracker," said Goggins.

"Great idea," said Zara.

"I do have them from time to time," said Goggins.

Zara hit him on the arm. "That's why I liked you so much in school when we first met."

"You did?" Goggins asked. "Oh, that makes me feel warm and fuzzy right in the midst of an impending battle."

Zara grinned. "Back to the screens, Dr. Goggins."

"Um, you two, sorry to interrupt. Again, where is everyone?" I asked.

"Sorry, Gabe. I've got one, two — we've got five private spaceships commanded by Mawzians, and then our good friends from the Heragi Empire make up the sixth ship," said Goggins.

"And we have four. The *Alyssia*, Jeb's ship the *Otessis*, Stoller and Alex on the *Ravena* and Honora with the Mawzian ship," I said.

"Not a fair fight, is it? Four to six," said Goggins.

"Open up comm links to everyone on their ships," I commanded.

"Copy that," replied Feti. "Comm links are open."

"Do all of those private ships the Mawzians pirated have advanced weapon systems?" I asked.

"That's affirmative, Gabe," said Feti.

"I guess rich people like guns, too," said Honora through her comm link.

"They have them for pirates," added Stoller from his ship.

"Gabe, we got it. Sending the info to our friends," said Goggins.

"Okay, listen up everyone. Zara and Goggins are sending you all navigational tracking of the Mawzians and their five ships. Take the closest one and tail it. Try not to engage, but if you have to, then your orders are to disable the ships only," I said.

"And who gets the extra ship?" asked Alex.

"We'll all have to share in that pleasure," said Jeb.

"Copy that," said Alex.

I looked on my screen and saw the closest Mawzian commandeered ship. It had already starting coming for us. It approached our starboard. It was a mid-size cruiser with only one gun turret at the top but also had four missile launchers on the bottom of its hull. It looked fast. Really fast.

"Gabe, we've got a torpedo lock on us," said Goggins.

"You see it, Gabe?" yelled Zara.

"I do," I replied, flying an evasive maneuver. I was drawing the Mawzians far enough away from the station not to expose it to possible torpedo damage. "Let's see how fast you are."

I pressed our accelerator and made it look like we were fleeing the station. It paused a bit. I knew the Mawzians were deciding to either come after me or double-team one of our team's ships.

Crap. I shouldn't have left so fast. I should have let them take a missile or gun shot to make them feel the taste of battle. To get their ego involved so they wouldn't want to let go once they started our dance of gun exchange.

That was the one difference that I could play with, their ego. They were still humanoids, after all, underneath all the cyborg coding. They weren't binary. They had feelings and didn't want to disappoint. I knew how that felt. And even with their mission and prime directive, that they couldn't delete or dissuade in their minds, they wouldn't want to fail.

I pulled back the accelerator and faked a stall.

They noticed. They started coming after the *Alyssia*.

"Gabe, we have a problem," said Zara.

I looked at my screen. The Mawzian cruiser barreled down on us.

What now?

19

____

"What is it, Zara?" I asked.

"We can only track the Mawzians' nanobots across so many yards. Seven hundred to be exact," she explained.

"We've basically lost tracking on the other ships, besides the one approaching," said Goggins.

"Copy that," I said. "Relay that to the other ships. Everyone needs to stay close then," I ordered.

"Which makes this a bit more like a knife fight," said Goggins.

The Mawzian-manned cruiser lost their missile lock on us when we accelerated, but they were getting close to another lock as they came flying behind us. I got out of our fake stall and began reviewing combat files in my directory. I kept flying some preliminary maneuvers that any novice pilot could do, but that was not going to hold them off for long.

"Gabe? What are you doing?" asked Zara.

"Loading a combat pilot program."

"Can you upload any faster?" said Goggins. "They've got another target lock on us."

"Hold on." I pulled out and reversed our engines and let them fly by us.

Our bodies heaved forward and then back. Goggins and Zara let out gasps of pain as their seat restrainers pulled against their bodies. Mine hurt too.

"Sorry," I said through the pain. "Upload completed."

The cruiser pulled around and got back on our tail. I followed the combat program's evasive procedures. For every move I made, they mirrored. For every change in direction, speed and dimensional change — they matched it just a millisecond after I triggered the change.

"Target lock — again," yelled Goggins.

I got us out of it — again.

This was not working.

"Gabe, you can't beat them," said Zara. "They have the same programs."

"They're following the programs to a T," I said.

"Right, so you need to improvise. Just as Ava and Damiel programmed you. That's your strength. Your superpower is that you're not robotic. You can't follow those programs anymore," explained Goggins.

I flew and thought. He was right. I was not human and I was not a cyborg, but I did have the ability to improvise.

"Got it," I said.

I headed back toward the Charbeaux Station as I put us in acceleration. The cruiser followed us and tried to get a missile lock.

As soon as we got within eyesight of our team, who were also in dogfights with the Mawzian-piloted ships, I got on the comms.

"Okay, everyone. These Mawzian pilots are playing by the book. Too close to their pilot programs. We need to change our strategy," I said.

"I was wondering why I couldn't lose them," said Honora.

"Back in the day, my pilot buddies and I used to play Hot Potato. Anyone remember that?" asked Stoller.

"An old favorite," said Jeb with a chuckle.

"For those of you too young to remember the game, lead your Mawzian in an infinity symbol. Then one of your buddies here will join in going the opposite way," explained Stoller.

"Copy that," said Honora.

"Jeb and I will start," said Stoller.

I watched as Stoller started a formation. The Mawzian close behind him followed him into the infinity formation. Then Jeb started in the opposite direction. They linked at the center of the symbol and came so close to each other that the target lock the Mawzian had was broken.

"Whew hee!" yelled Stoller.

"That was fun. Let's do it again, partner," said Jeb.

"Here we go," said Stoller.

I started the *Alyssia* on the beginning of our own infinity figure. "Are you ready, Honora?"

Honora started to move in the opposite direction. "Yes, here I go," she said. "Only a slight problem. I've got two Mawzian ships on my tail."

Honora and I came together and narrowly missed each other in the middle.

"Whoa, that was close," yelled Goggins as he watched Honora race by us.

"But it worked," said Zara. "Our Mawzians lost their target lock on us."

"Hey guys, the Heragi ship following me is falling out of the formation," said Honora.

"What's he doing?" I asked.

"He's not having any of it," said Jeb. "He probably played this at the Academy. Blasted."

"He's got a target lock on me," yelled Honora. "What do I do?"

"Get out of there!" yelled Stoller. "Break out of the pattern. Now!"

I watched as Honora, pulled out of the formation and headed around the station. Then I saw Jeb pull out of his pattern and start tailing the Heragi ship.

"Jeb just put a target lock on the Heragis," said Goggins, looking up.

"We said no target locks," I reminded him.

"Not correct. You said no target locks on Mawzians. These are Heragi soldiers trying to kill my niece," said Jeb.

"Jeb, the woman and little girl are on that ship with the Mawzians," I yelled. "Stand down."

"Blasted. Okay, targeting their engines only," said Jeb.

Two missiles launched from Jeb's ship, the *Otessis*. One missed the Heragi ship. The second hit their engines. The Heragi ship tumbled out of its path of pursuit on Honora. Their target lock on her stopped.

I looked in my monitor and out my window. Honora came around the other side of the station.

"Crap, I can't shake this one," cried Honora.

"They got a lock on her," yelled Goggins.

"Hold on, Honora," called Jeb.

The Mawzians trailing Honora's ship launched their missile. It hit the stern. Her ship was damaged and she was losing control of it.

"Honora, get out of there," yelled Jeb.

"Copy that," replied Honora.

Within seconds, a small shape in an environmental suit leaped off the ship as it broke apart.

The Mawzian ship that shot the missile closed in on Honora floating in space.

"What are they doing?" asked Jeb.

"They're going to try to grab her," said Stoller.

"I got a target lock on me. Who can get to Honora?" yelled Jeb.

"Target lock on us, too, Gabe," said Goggins.

"Stoller?" I tried.

"I got two on my tail right now that I'm dodging," said Stoller.

I watched Honora flip over and over in space. She tried to stabilize with nitrogen pulses from her spacesuit. She leveled off. She looked around and saw the ship coming after her.

We couldn't let them take her.

"Gabe, we have another ship coming into our perimeter," said Zara.

"Who is it?" I asked.

Then a female voice broke into our comms. "Mind if we step in, everyone?"

A sleek navy destroyer flew into our view. It was Oliverian.

"Bre? Is that you?" asked Stoller.

"Yes, and I've got someone else onboard," said Admiral Bre.

"Bre!" yelled Stoller. "Whoo, good to hear your voice."

A skiff departed from the Oliverian navy destroyer. "Hey, Stoller, I'm going in for the girl," said Anjori.

"Glad you're with us," said Stoller.

We all watched as Anjori flew out. She swooped in and launched a spray of gunfire toward the ship trying to grab Honora.

"Just a little scare tactic," said Anjori as she slowed to get near Honora. The skiff's port door opened. Honora tried to direct her body toward the door but was having problems.

"Blasted, the jets are jamming," said Honora as she struggled.

"Hey, I'm in a bit of a jam, folks. I got two target locks on me. Anyone feel like helping me out over here?" Stoller dove in and around the station.

"I got you covered, buddy," said a new male voice.

"Tristan!" yelled Stoller.

Tristan flew by us in an Oliverian navy fighter ship. He swooped down and fired his guns on the two Mawzian ships trailing Stoller. He hit their gun turrets and put both ships out of commission for firing gun rounds. Tristan took another loop around and assaulted their missile hatches.

"Great shot!" Goggins fist-pumped.

"Why thank you," said Tristan.

"I'll be honest, kid, I didn't know you had it in you."

"What, to knock those two ships out?" asked Tristan.

"No, to save my sorry butt," laughed Stoller.

"Honora's jets aren't working. I'm going out to get her," said Anjori.

We watched as a figure attached to a line came out of the skiff. It was Anjori reaching for Honora. She was within thirty yards and closing. She was getting closer. Honora started spinning again. Anjori had to carefully calculate grabbing Honora or they both would have an unpleasant reel in to the skiff.

Anjori waited and then lunged for Honora. They crashed together. We heard them both grunt with pain.

They began to spin, but Anjori had a firm grasp on Honora.

"Hooking her onto my line," yelled Anjori. She used her nitrogen jets to move them in the direction of the skiff. Anjori had to reel them in fast to get tension on the line before they rammed into the ship.

"Get it under control, Anjori. You're almost there," said Tristan.

Anjori straightened them out and the line tensed up.

"Got it," said a breathless Anjori. She pulled Honora into her skiff.

"Gabe, we have the code to change the Mawzians' prime directive," said a familiar voice.

"Ava?" I said.

"Yes, and Damiel. We're here with the Oliverians. We hitched a ride with Admiral Bre," said Ava.

"Hi, Gabe. Hi, kids," said Damiel.

"Great," said Zara. "We can send you the nanobot chip information and navigation trackers for you to code to."

"Thank you, Zara," said Ava.

Zara sent the data packages to Admiral Bre's ship.

Stoller, Jeb and I were still dodging around the station with the Mawzian ships trying to put target locks on us.

"Hurry, Ava. I'm getting pretty tired of these games with the Mawzians without being able to blow them into a million pieces," said Jeb.

"Yes, you've shown great restraint," teased Zara.

"Damiel, what's going to happen to the Mawzians once their prime directive is changed?" asked Goggins.

"They'll essentially reboot. The directive will be changed, but they will still have all their robotic code and programs from Gabe and the gifts from the children," Damiel explained.

"Reboot?" said Zara. "How long does that take?"

"Two to four minutes," replied Damiel.

"We need to lead the Mawzians out into space, away from the station, or their pilots could unintentionally crash their ships into the station when they are rebooting," I said.

"Copy that," said Stoller.

"Leading them out," said Jeb.

We all pulled our ships away from Charbeaux Station out to deep space. We weaved and dodged until we received word from Ava.

"It's done. The code is uploading to the Mawzians' nanobots now," Ava said.

"Hot blasters!" said Stoller.

"Great job, Ava and Damiel," said Jeb.

I slowed our ship down.

Zara and Goggins jumped out of their seats, hugged and let out some celebratory cries. They came up to me.

"Well?" said Zara.

I looked up. "What?"

She gave me a stern look. "You need to stand up."

I stood. And then she hugged me. I wrapped my hands around her and hugged her back. She pulled away and laughed. "That was awkward, but it worked."

Yeah, I thought so, too.

Goggins held up his hand for a high five. I gave him one. He smiled. Talia came up and hugged me. She then took a seat in the co-commander chair. Humans like to touch. It felt good. I felt the warm feeling in my chest. I hadn't felt that in a while.

I turned around and stared at the ships the Mawzians were in. They had stopped pursuing us. We waited for the minutes to go by until the Mawzians rebooted.

"Will they remember what they did?" asked Alex between the long silences.

Anjori answered, "Yes. But it will be hazy."

"Someone will have to explain this all to them," said Zara.

"We'll have them land back at the station and take them in for a debriefing," said Damiel.

"Their reboots should all be complete," said Ava.

"Feti, give me a comms link to all the Mawzian piloted ships," I said.

"Copy that, Gabe. One moment," said Feti. "You are linked to all of their comms."

"Gabe? Do you mind if I take the lead on this?" asked Jeb.

I paused. That made sense. After all, he was a rebel commander, and I was not.

"Sure, Jeb. It's all yours," I said. "Feti, give Jeb's ship the open comms link."

"Copy that, Gabe," said Feti.

Talia sent me a thought. *We need to go get Meeor and Belin.*

I nodded and accelerated the *Alyssia* back to the station. I sent a direct comm to Stoller. "Could use your help with getting the woman and girl."

"Copy that," responded Stoller. "Tristan, want to tag along?"

"I'll beat you to them," said Tristan, and he took off.

"Show off," said Stoller.

As we pulled away, Jeb began his introduction to the Mawzians.

"To all Mawzians. This is Jebediah Kell. I speak for all the Heragi rebel leaders in hoping that everyone is safe and healthy on your spaceships. Some of you may be confused or disorientated. We are sending you coordinates for landing back on the substation at the planet-port. We will greet all of you there. We are your friends, not your enemy. The Heragis won't be torturing you anymore."

Stoller and I sped back to the last spot we left the Heragi ship. The soldiers by now must have realized that Meeor had a coding reboot. But we didn't know if Belin still had her prime directive or not.

"It looks like their skiff hasn't been launched," said Stoller as he flew close to the ship.

"Let's open a comm to them," I said.

"Copy that," said Stoller.

"Feti, get me a comm link to the Mawzian ship," I asked.

"Copy that, Gabe. Go ahead," said Feti.

"This is Gabe, commander of the *Alyssia*. Please identify yourselves," I said.

After a few moments, a solider spoke. "We know who you are."

"Good," I said, not knowing what to say. I remembered that Ava uploaded a hostage negotiation program in my directory tied to my mission back at the lab. I went into my visor view and looked it up. I downloaded it. Ah, that was better. I had all the tactics and strategies that should make this successful.

"We will let you leave on your skiff, just leave the Mawzian woman and child," I began.

Anjori's skiff arrived on the scene and was docking on the Heragi ship.

"What's happening?" said Zara.

"Indeed," said a dumbstruck Goggins.

"Gabe, we got this," said Anjori.

"What?" I stumbled for words.

"We're making a trade. This was already negotiated," said Tristan.

"What was already negotiated?" asked Stoller.

"We're giving them our skiff. And we get the Mawzians," said Tristan.

"How come you didn't include us in the comms on that?" asked a confused Stoller.

"We are also giving them Foxwell," said Tristan.

"What?" yelled Jeb. "Whose call was that?"

"Our call, Jebediah. The Oliverians'," said Tristan.

"I find this hard to swallow," I said.

"It's true, Gabe. We have Foxwell," said Admiral Bre.

"And you're just going to let him loose?" I asked.

"It's a trade. A direct order from Swina Oliverian," said Admiral Bre.

"It's the wrong move," said Jeb.

"I have to agree with Jeb on this one, Bre," said Stoller.

"You're all soldiers who don't understand the diplomatic process," said Tristan. "Every war is ended by diplomacy. Without it, we would have ongoing battles until no planet or substation was left in this galaxy."

"The girl. We didn't give her the shot. She still has her prime directive," said Stoller.

"We have the girl. We'll take care of it. She's in safe hands," said Anjori.

We all watched in silence as Anjori's skiff docked. Foxwell was on that skiff. I hoped he was handcuffed.

The Heragi soldiers took command of the skiff and left Meeor and Belin on their ship for Anjori to pilot back to Charbeaux Station.

I pulled back and prepared the *Alyssia* to land at the planetport.

"I can't believe they gave Foxwell back," said Goggins.

"It may have been a good call," said Zara.

Talia's spoke through her arm comm. "Meeor and Belin are safe. It *was* a good call."

I didn't respond.

I let Talia's words sink in. My chest warmed.

It was the right call.

20

———————

We all sat in the Charbeaux Station planet-port's ops room. It looked over all the incoming and exiting ships. The station still impressed me, and I stood there with the Kell children looking at the busy transport center.

Leroy sat near Stoller, all bandaged up. I approached him and extended my hand. Leroy had never shaken the hand of a robot, I surmised, but he took my hand.

"Thank you," I said.

"You're welcome. I hope this is the first and last time that we have to meet under these circumstances," he said with a smile.

"I agree." I took a seat.

"Come on, it wasn't that bad," Stoller said. "I wiped out all of your quinker debt to me."

Leroy laughed. "That's true."

"But I'd like a rematch tonight at the Blue Edger bar," said Stoller.

"Here we go again," replied Leroy.

I looked at the Kell children, who sat with their parents. Alex had grown into a fine soldier. I knew he didn't want to go back to Zaradorba.

Stoller leaned over to me. "Alex is a good kid. He's green and all but a good co-pilot and a heck of a gunner in the turret."

I nodded. I knew where this was going.

"I'm going to talk to Ava and Damiel about him taking the *Ravena* for a while," explained Stoller.

"For what purpose?" I asked.

"He can keep an eye on my ship. I need to set some things straight with Kaleb Kron," he said.

"The bounty hunter."

"Yes."

"I wouldn't think the Kells would want their son mixed up with clearing your name," I said.

"I don't know. I'm an innocent man. I heard the galaxy courts have robot judges now. So I think I have a fair chance of reasoning with them. I mean you and I got along all right, didn't we?"

I think he was teasing me.

I shrugged. "I guess we did."

Stoller laughed his deep belly laugh. "Anyway, Alex can borrow my ship, and I was wondering if you would come with me to the Justice Station while I clear up this whole bounty situation. How about it?"

I had nothing better to do. "Sounds good. I'm sure Goggins and Zara would be happy to join too."

"I was counting on it," said Stoller with a grin.

Alex sat down next to us.

"What did they say?" asked Stoller.

"They're not happy, but they said as long as I check in with them regularly, they'll allow it," explained Alex.

Stoller slapped Alex's shoulder. "Now, when I wrap up all my legal stuff, I want the *Ravena* back without a scratch, okay?".

"Hey, I'm going to have an expert pilot with me. Honora is coming, too," said Alex.

"She is?" I asked.

"Yes, and Talia," said Alex.

"Wow, your mother is loosening up, huh?" I asked.

"Just a bit," said Alex with a grin.

Talia sent me a thought from across the room. *Alex, Honora and I are going on a trip in Stoller's ship.*

So I heard. How are your parents taking it?

Dad's sort of okay with it. Mom isn't happy, but she's allowing it.

Great. She'll probably blame me for that, too.

Don't be so hard on yourself.

A pain hit my chest. I turned to glance over to Talia.

Our conversation was interrupted by Jeb, who called our meeting to order.

I glanced around the room. Admiral Bre, Anjori and Tristan sat together at a table. Ava and Damiel sat with Honora.

Goggins and Zara sat together reviewing their coders as they were still monitoring the Mawzians' vital signs in the room next door where they rested. Vincent, the Mawzian, sat at the table as a representative of his people.

Synthia sat alone until Talia came up to her and held her hand.

"Everyone, it's time to discuss building an alliance against the Heragi Empire," started Jeb. "For two years, the rebel base has been Zaradorba, where we have assembled a sizable resistance army, but it's not enough. We need friends. We need allies."

"Swina and the Oliverian Council have approved us joining an alliance," said Admiral Bre.

"Thank you, Admiral," said Jeb.

"Two planets against the whole Heragi Empire?" said Stoller with a grunt. "How many planets do the Heragi control? Thirty or forty? I lost count over the last decade."

"Yes, it's formidable," said Jeb.

"That is why we're asking some of you to go to planets that

you know. Talk to their leaders. Ask them to join us," said Anjori.

"It would have helped if you didn't give back the Heragis' most senior general," said Stoller.

"We had our reasons," said Anjori.

"I heard," said Stoller under his breath but loud enough for all to hear.

"Synthia has agreed to take the Mawzians back to her home planet to train them on their new gifts," said Jeb.

"Once we have completed our training, we want to fight," said Vincent. "But not only the Heragi. We need to end slave trading on Mawzi."

Everyone agreed.

Stoller leaned over to me and whispered, "I'd hate to be on the Mawzian government board. They have a bunch of the most angry and skilled cybs coming their way. And they deserve it."

I had to agree with Stoller. The Mawzian cybs were unique. As a fighting unit, they could easily become the most powerful army in the galaxy. And with procreation, they could create a super race.

"It's risky for governments and planets to join an alliance," said Zara. "Even if they do hate the Heragi, they play the game of tolerance, so they won't be next on their hit list."

"You're right. But you have witnessed what the Heragi Empire can do. We all must try," said Jeb.

Zara looked at me and Goggins. "Well?"

"Of course," said Goggins. Zara put her hand on his shoulder.

I nodded. "But Stoller wants us to help him with something first."

"Stoller? What's the problem?" asked Tristan.

Stoller got up. "I have things I need to do."

"Ah, the old Stoller returns, putting yourself first," said Tristan.

"Listen, I need to get some personal things taken care of," he explained.

"And then you can go to Deragi and ask for their assistance in the cause?" asked Jeb.

Stoller looked out the window into space and then down at the planet-port. I reviewed his bio-metrics. They were lowering. I didn't think he wanted to leave the station. Or perhaps he just didn't want to go back home.

Stoller hung his head and then took a deep breath. "Afterward. Yes, I will go back to Deragi. I will ask them to join the alliance."

"Good, that's good," said Jeb.

"Anjori, Bre, Tristan, where are you off to?" asked Stoller. "To Mawzi with Vincent to serve up some revenge for imprisoning Anjori for ten years?"

Anjori stared at Stoller and then answered, "No, the Mawzians will take care of their own. We are going to deep space, farther into the Edge.

"Why? What's out there?" asked Stoller.

"That's where Anjori was going when her ship crashed on Mawzi. She wasn't targeting the Mawzians. It was an emergency landing, not a spy mission," said Tristan.

"Anyway, the details are above your clearance level, Stoller," said Admiral Bre.

"I thought we were all friends here. I mean, I did save Anjori," emphasized Stoller.

"It's for everyone's protection that we keep where we're going and why we are going secret," said Tristan.

"Fine. Good luck to you. The Edge is, well, the Edge," said Stoller with a wink. "But you know that."

"And I've been re-instated. It's General Anjori to you."

"Yes, General. Can I buy you a drink after this meeting?" Stoller said with a wink.

He was incorrigible. I liked him for that. I think everyone did. Maybe not Anjori. She just stared at him.

"You can buy me a drink," said Tristan.

"Okay, fine," said Stoller.

There seemed to be a harshness in Anjori's face. Who could blame her? And she might have always been that way. She was a general, after all. And her DNA now had, let's say, robotic tendencies.

"Okay, let's continue, everyone. Ava and Damiel will return to Zaradorba where we will keep our rebel headquarters for now," said Jeb.

"And the Kell children?" I asked.

Jeb snapped back. He had forgotten about his nieces and nephew, but I hadn't. Jeb turned and looked at each one of them. "I assumed they would go back with Ava and Damiel."

Zara laughed. "That figures. Those kids are more grown up than you think."

"And more powerful," said Synthia.

Honora exchanged a look with her siblings and stood up. "We have discussed it. And shared it with our parents. They give us permission. Although I think we would go anyway. Sorry, Mom and Dad. I don't mean to be disrespectful."

"We know, children, with the gifts you all have, you need to forge your own path," said Ava.

Was Ava actually letting go and allowing her children to spread their wings? My heart warmed a bit.

"We've decided to go back to Heragi," said Honora.

"Please don't get my ship banged up," said Stoller.

"We won't. Geez, quiet, Stoller," snapped Honora.

Everyone in the room objected but especially their Uncle Jebediah.

"What? That's out of the question!" yelled Jeb. He realized his emotions were too strong, and he tried to speak calmly. "Ava and Damiel, you are allowing this? It could jeopardize our resistance if they get caught again."

"Listen to them. They have a plan," said Ava.

"What's their plan?" I asked.

Honora threw a diagram from her comm device up to a hologram view above the conference table so all could see it. It was a rendering of Heragi and its sol system.

"Some of you may believe that the ancient gifts my brother, me and Talia have are one in a million or five million, but they're not. After discussion with my parents and with Synthia, we've concluded there are more children and adults like us down on Heragi," explained Honora.

She waved her hand and the Heragi planet magnified and spun. We could see the various continents. Honora waved her hand again. Approximately one hundred blue dots popped up.

"Before my parents left, they dug into birth medical records for the past fifty years. They made a directory of Heragians who have some of the same DNA strands me and my siblings have," she continued.

"Amazing," said Zara.

"And dangerous if those people get into the Heragi military's hands," said Jeb.

"Exactly. That's why we're going back. To find them. Later, we will assemble with all of you about an extraction mission," said Honora.

Everyone kept looking at the twirling planet with blue dots.

"What do you say?" said Honora.

"That's a big job, kid" said Stoller as he scratched his chin.

"And that is why we need more planets to join our alliance," said Jeb.

"Uncle, do you approve?"

"Yes, but the details will need to be hashed out, agreed?"

"Agreed," said Honora with a smile on her face.

"Be on alert that we may be calling on any or all of you for assistance for future missions, at the beginning, middle or end of our journey to free this galaxy," said Jeb.

Everyone nodded and agreed.

If I could let out a deep breath at that moment, I would have. How does such a small girl create such big plans? I reviewed all the strategic scenarios and probabilities in my head. This was going to be complicated. Much bigger than the mission we just completed of extracting Synthia, Anjori and the Mawzians.

Goggins cleared his throat. "And what is the name of our alliance?"

"The *cyborg loving edgers*?" offered Stoller.

"Stoller, behave," said Zara.

"I've been thinking of a name. How is the Federation of Free Planets?" said Jeb as he looked around the room for feedback.

"The FFP," said Admiral Bre.

"Yes, I like it. Freedom is our foundation," said Vincent.

Everyone smiled.

"If I had some gin, I would toast to freedom, too," said Stoller.

"Okay, then let's begin the first meeting of the Federation of Free Planets," said Jeb. "We will all be the founding board members. Planets that join will be allowed a seat at the table."

Everyone nodded.

We finished discussing all the pertinent next steps and orders of the FFP, and our meeting came to an end. I looked around the room and wondered when I would see everyone next. A small pain hit my chest. I wished I could keep us in this room for a while longer but knew that was not possible.

I looked at each of the Kell children. I was glad we were all here. Together. Ava glanced at me and smiled. I missed her most of all, even though she was right in front of me. I nodded to her.

Stoller suggested we all head to the Blue Edger bar to toast to freedom and our new alliance. Everyone agreed we should seal the deal with some more collegiality. As we proceeded through the Charbeaux Station on the way to the bar, I was able to take in the enjoyable architecture of the spinning sub-station in space. It still amazed me. I could live here, I thought, for a long time. But that would have to wait.

Talia ran up to walk with me, and she sent me a thought. *I was thinking, Gabe.*

Yes, Talia?

Mom and Dad created you, right?

Yes.

And Mom and Dad created me.

Yes.

That makes us brother and sister, right? We're siblings.

I thought about it.

Then Talia began to laugh. *Right?*

Yes, I guess you're right.

But I'm older. So, you're my little brother.

But I'm bigger.

Yes, but I'm older.

I started to grunt laugh with her. *I guess you're right, again.*

Older sisters are always right. Honora taught me that.

We walked down the hall together.

THE END

If you enjoyed this adventure, you can read more about Gabe and the team in JUSTICE, Book 3 in the Rogue Robot series.

Author Notes

Dear Reader,

Thank you for reading CYBS - Book 2 in the Rogue Robot Series! I hope you enjoyed the book.

I love writing about Gabe, our sentient robot. Over the past year I've planned out the series and learn more about Gabe and all the characters with each book that comes to fruition. I'm excited to show you where they all end up.

Want a little more? "Justice" is Book 3 in the Rogue Robot series and is available to buy now! Continue reading the adventures with Gabe and his team as they take on the Heragi Empire.

Also, I've written a free bonus prequel novella e-book with Gabe, Ava, Damiel and Goggins called *Robots Don't Cry*. It takes place a few months before "Rogue" Book 1 starts. You can get this free prequel novella e-book, along with updates on new books in the series and future bonus materials by hitting this link and **signing up for my newsletter** on my website at **www. MegFoster.com.**

If you really liked the book and want to read more Rogue Robot adventures, please consider leaving a review for Rogue and share the title with your friends. I'd appreciate it greatly! Thank you!

-Meg Foster

Books by Meg Foster

Rogue Robot Series:

ROBOTS DON'T CRY (prequel novella ebook)*
ROGUE (Book 1)
CYBS (Book 2)
JUSTICE (Book 3)
HARMONIX (Book 4)
TRINITY (Book 5)
CODA (Book 6)

*Only available when signing up for
Meg's newsletter.

This series is meant to be read in order.

About the Author

Sci-fi author **Meg Foster** explores the pitfalls and triumphs of human nature and technology. She reaches out to make us think and experience a wide range of emotions through her unique voice. Meg's meaningful and mirthful writing delivers stories we can savor and enjoy.

In addition to writing novels, Meg is a filmmaker and wrote, directed and produced the comedy/drama film "Stealing Roses" starring John Heard and Cindy Williams.

She was born in Detroit, Michigan and received a B.A. in Film Production from Southern Illinois University at Carbondale. When she isn't writing or enjoying the lakes and mountains near her home in the Pacific Northwest, you can find her online at www.MegFoster.com.

Also find Meg on Facebook where she has a private FB Group where readers come together, have fun, discuss the series, and speak directly with her at www.facebook.com/TheMegFoster.

Thank you for reading!